A Thousand Ways Home

Lou Mindar

Driftless House Publishing

Library of Congress Cataloging-in-Publication Data
Mindar, Lou (1959 -)
A Thousand Ways Home / Lou Mindar. – First Edition.
[Novel]
Pages cm
ISBN 978-0-9972488-3-8
Paperback edition

"There are a thousand ways to kneel and kiss the
ground; there are a thousand ways to go home."
— Rumi

A Thousand Ways Home

Section 1

*Chicago
(1908-1920)*

Chapter 1
(1908)

The sand burned my tender feet as we walked across the beach. My mother carried the beach bag with our towels, some sandwiches that our negro maid, Sally, made for us, and a blanket that we would sit on once we got to our usual place on the sand.

"Pick your feet up faster, Henry," my mother said. "The sand won't have as much time to burn them."

I did as I was instructed, but it didn't seem to help.

As my mother tried to prod me along, my brother, Philip, ran ahead, oblivious to my burning feet. I was eight years old. Philip was eleven. My brother loved to swim in Lake Michigan on hot summer days. He shared my mother's love for the beach. Although I didn't hate the beach, being there didn't thrill me the way it did my mother and Philip. I just wanted to spend time with the two of them. At my young age, they were my world.

We found our spot and my mother spread the blanket out on the sand. She and I sat on the blanket, but Philip ran down to the lake's edge to get his feet wet and check the temperature of the water. He stood in the ankle-deep water for a few moments, then joined us on the blanket.

"It's warming up," he said. "It's not as cold as it was last week."

We had come to the beach the previous week, but the month of May had been unusually cold, and the water hadn't warmed up enough yet to swim. Now that we were into June, it was beginning to warm.

"Why don't you eat the lunch Sally made for us before you go in the water?" my mother asked.

"I'm not hungry. I want to go swimming." Philip shifted from one foot to the other in the warm sand.

Mother gave him a stern look, then relented. She smiled. "All right. Go ahead," she said. "But stay near shore and be careful."

Philip turned and ran toward the water.

My mother pulled two sandwiches out of the beach bag and handed one to me. Sally had used the leftover chicken from the previous night's dinner to make chicken salad. I took a big bite and got mayonnaise on each side of my mouth. My mother wiped it off with a napkin.

"Since you're not practicing piano today, you're going to have to practice twice as hard tomorrow."

My mother was adamant that I practice every day. When I complained a few months earlier, she told me why she was so insistent. "You and your brother each have your own special gifts. Philip is athletic. He's a talented runner, and he excels at track and field."

I was looking at the floor. She put her finger under my chin and tilted my head up, making sure I looked her in the eyes.

"You're a gifted musician who has become a wonderful piano player. We need to nurture the gifts we've been given, Henry. We can't let them go to waste. That would be a sin. That's why I want you to practice every day. Do you understand?"

I nodded. I thought I understood.

After our discussion, I felt special, like I had been given a gift that others—most importantly, Philip—had not been given. I would have preferred to be as fast and athletic as my brother but being a "gifted musician" was good too. So, I began to practice every day—well, almost every day—so I didn't waste my gift.

"Why doesn't Father ever come to the beach with us?" I asked.

"He's very busy with work," she said. "Otherwise, I'm sure he'd join us."

My mother and father had both grown up in Indiana. My father's father was a farmer, and I was born on his farm. But a few years after my birth, my grandfather died, leaving the farm to us. A few weeks after the funeral, my father sold the farm and moved us to Chicago. He invested the proceeds in the Chicago Butter and Egg Board. The investment made us wealthy, and his job as a broker kept him away from home most of the time. Mother and Sally raised Philip and me. Father made occasional appearances.

Out in the lake, Philip splashed around in waist-deep water, spinning in circles and occasionally plunging his head beneath the surface. Mother watched him from the blanket while she talked to me.

My mother was much different than my father. She was kind and caring. She loved art and music, and she made an effort to spend time with Philip and me. My father was all about work. He didn't spend much time with my brother or me. He rarely attended Philip's track meets or my piano recitals. In fact, I had two piano recitals in the past year. My father didn't attend either, but my mother attended both.

Yet, I took my mother for granted and wanted desperately for my father to spend time with me or say a kind word about my schoolwork or piano playing. I loved my mother, but I felt something akin to worship for my father. I wanted to be like him, despite the fact that it was my mother who took care of me, supported me, and was there when I needed anything.

My mother took a bite of her sandwich. She watched Philip as he dove into the water, then resurfaced, just to dive again. "Wouldn't it be fun to…"

My mother jumped up from the blanket and stood, watching Philip. I looked out at the lake but couldn't see him. Mother took a step toward the lake, then another.

"Philip," she called loudly. She took another step, then began running. When she did, she dropped her sandwich in the sand. She got to the water's edge and called Philip's name again, then ran into the lake. She squatted down in the waist-deep water, her arms feeling around under the surface for my brother. She moved out deeper, and dove under, out of my sight.

I was frightened for both Philip and my mother, but I stayed glued to the blanket, still eating my sandwich. I have never been able to understand my inability to stand up and help my mother find my brother. It has been a scar on my soul since the day it happened.

A man ran by, kicking sand up as he ran. He went to the water's edge and stared at the spot where my mother had gone underwater. When she didn't come back up to the surface, he ran fully clothed into the lake. I remained on the blanket.

People began to gather near the water's edge. When the police arrived, the man who had gone into the water came back up onto the beach. He talked to the police and gestured toward the lake. Some firemen joined the police and rowed a small boat out into the water. They rowed the boat back and forth along the beach for what must have been an hour or more. I was still on the blanket when they rowed to shore and unloaded two bodies onto the sand.

The police walked along the beach asking if anyone knew the people they had pulled from the lake. When they asked me, I was still on the blanket, unable to move.

"Do you know those people?" The policeman pointed toward the bodies.

I nodded.

Three seagulls fought over the remains of the sandwich my mother had dropped in the sand. They screeched loudly. When someone walked near the birds, they flew off down the beach, one of them carrying a chuck of discarded bread.

The policeman knelt beside me. "You do now, do you?" he asked. "Who might they be?"

I stared down at the blanket.

"It's all right, son. We just want to know who they are."

I looked at the policeman, my head tilted to the side. He smiled and nodded his reassurance.

"Mother and Philip." My voice seemed to come from far away.

He asked a few more questions and I answered as best I could. "You did good, son," the policeman said. "You stay here. I'll be right back."

I stayed on the blanket and watched as the firemen loaded my mother and Philip onto a cart, then wheel them away. I wanted to go with them, but the policeman told me to stay on the blanket.

It was almost dark when I saw my father walking across the sand in his suit and top hat. A policeman pointed at me, and my father came to where I sat.

"Henry, are you alright?" There was a flatness to his voice.

I stood and ran to him, hugging his legs. He put a hand on my back but didn't hug me. I hugged him tighter, needing his embrace.

"We have to go home." He released his tepid hug.

I didn't understand. Did he know about Mother and Philip? Were they going to be alright? "Where's Mother?" I asked.

"Your mother…" He looked out at the lake and shook his head. "Let's go home."

Chapter 2
(1913)

I was in the kitchen looking for a snack when Sally came into the room. She was a dark-skinned negro with a short, rotund body. Next to my mother, Sally was the kindest person I had ever met.

"What are you looking for?" she asked.

"I want a snack. Some cookies or something."

"You're going to ruin your appetite before dinner. We're having pot roast tonight."

It was Sunday. The only day of the week I knew I was going to have dinner with my father. Most nights, he was still at his office, working, while I was home having dinner by myself. Occasionally, I'd take my food into the kitchen and eat with Sally, which was inappropriate. My father would have gotten angry had he known, but I was often lonely and didn't want to eat alone. Besides, to me, Sally was like family.

"Aren't you supposed to be practicing piano?" she asked.

"I did already."

"I heard you playing for ten minutes," she said. "You need to practice more than that. Your mother would want you practicing at least thirty minutes."

Sally knew that by invoking my mother, she could guilt me into practicing more. Plus, she was right. I had only practiced for ten minutes before I went hunting for a snack.

"Play me one of those songs I like," Sally said.

Sally loved Scott Joplin rags, and often asked me to play them for her, although she didn't know the names of any of his songs.

"I learned a new one," I said.

Sally's face broke into a smile, and she followed me out to the piano. I found the sheet music in the wooden piano bench, then sat in front of the keyboard.

"Tell me if you like this one." I studied the sheet music for a moment, then started playing Joplin's "Kismet Rag" for her.

I had only played a few moments when my father came storming into the piano room. "Stop. Stop playing. What is that noise?"

"It's Scott Joplin." My voice was small and sheepish.

"Oh, Mr. Ross, that's my fault," Sally said. "I asked him to play that song."

"Sally, why don't you go check on dinner. I want to talk to Henry."

Sally turned away from the piano and waddled into the kitchen.

"It's enough that I have to hear you play Chopin or Beethoven when I'm trying to relax, but this music, this…" He struggled to find the word he wanted to use. "This filth. You make our home sound like a backroad tavern."

"I'm sorry, Father. I was just…" There was nothing I could say to smooth this over with him. It seemed that everything I did irritated him. It felt like the mere sight of me could set him off, my very existence an affront to him.

"Playing piano was your mother's idea." He lowered his voice and was calmer. "It's nice that you've continued playing, even after her…with her not here. But I can't allow that jungle music in this house. If you insist on continuing to play the piano, the only thing I ask of you is that you do it when I'm not here. Is that too much to ask?"

"No, Father." I fought back tears. My father was home so seldom that finding time to play was not going to be a problem. But what upset me was the complete disregard he had for my love for the piano, what my mother had called my "gift." Dismissing my piano playing was akin to dismissing me. A tear rolled down my cheek and I quickly wiped it away.

Seeing me cry seemed to jolt him. "Oh, I didn't…Henry, I…" He stared at me for a moment, then turned and walked out of the piano room.

We didn't speak at dinner that night. I had nothing to say. I felt rejected. It's how I had felt ever since my mother and Philip drowned. My father didn't like to be around me. I always felt uneasy around him, and I felt that he blamed me for the deaths of my mother and brother.

After they died, whenever I'd talk about my mother or Philip, my father would change the subject or simply ignore my question. I wanted to talk about them, but he refused, sometimes leaving the room to avoid a conversation. He made me feel guilty for wanting to remember them and talk about them.

His way of dealing with my mother and brother's deaths was to ignore the subject altogether. He never discussed their deaths and rarely brought up their names. I wanted to remember them. He seemed to want to forget that they ever existed.

"May I be excused?" I asked.

My father looked up from his meal, but before he could say anything, Sally, who was standing in the corner waiting to serve us, spoke up.

"You've barely eaten any of your food," she said.

I looked at Sally, then at my plate. "I'm not very hungry."

"You're excused," my father said. He stared at me and seemed to want to say more, but I pushed my chair back and stood to leave.

"He's a growing boy, Mr. Ross. He needs to eat his food," Sally said.

"That will be all, Sally" my father said.

Chapter 3
(1915)

My father paced around the kitchen, looking over Sally's shoulder and talking to her while she tried to concentrate on cooking our meal.

"Mr. Ross, your guests should be here shortly," Sally said. "Why don't you go out to the front door to wait for them?"

Father looked at his watch. "It is almost time." He left the kitchen.

"What's with him?" I asked. "I've never seen him like that." It was a weeknight, which already made my father's presence at home unusual. His behavior made things even stranger.

"He just wants to make sure everything is ready for dinner," Sally said. "And you're not. You need to go upstairs and get dressed."

"Dressed? I am dressed."

"Oh no you're not," Sally said. "Your father wants you in a suit and tie tonight. I have everything laid out on your bed."

"What's so special about these people that I have to wear a suit and tie?" It was unusual for us to have guests for dinner, but on the rare occasion when we had company, I was never required to wear a suit.

"You'll see. Now go get ready."

I went upstairs. Just as Sally said, my suit was on the bed, along with a white button-down shirt and a tie. I got changed, and as I approached the stairway, I heard unfamiliar voices downstairs. I peered around the corner and saw a woman with strawberry blond hair, and two kids, both younger than me. My father was helping the woman take off her coat.

As I walked down the stairs, my father glanced up and saw me.

"There he is. Come down and join us, Henry." Father's voice was unusually pleasant and friendly.

The woman smiled as I descended the stairs. The youngest of the kids—a girl—hid behind the woman.

"Henry, this is Margaret Van Ohlen. Margaret, this is my son, Henry."

"It's nice to meet you, Mrs. Van Ohlen," I said.

"It's nice to meet you, Henry." She put her arm around the older of the children. "This is my son, Roger. He's twelve years old." Roger approached me and offered his hand.

"It's a pleasure to make your acquaintance," he said.

I shook his hand. He may have only been twelve, but he talked and acted like an adult. "You too," I said.

"And this shy little thing is Sarah. She's ten." Margaret moved Sarah in front of her. When she did, Sarah blushed and looked down at the floor.

"Hi, Sarah," I said.

Sarah remained quiet until her mother nudged her.

"Hi."

"Dinner should be ready in a few minutes," my father said. "Until then, why don't we all go into the living room." He led the way and we all followed. When Mrs. Van Ohlen and the children were seated, my father excused himself so he could hang up the woman's coat.

There was an uncomfortable silence until Mrs. Van Ohlen finally spoke. "You have a lovely home, Henry."

"Thank you," I said reflexively. "I'm going to check on dinner." I rushed out of the living room to the relative safety of the kitchen.

"What are you doing in here?" Sally asked.

"I'm just…Who are these people?" I asked.

"Didn't your father introduce you?"

"Mrs. Van Ohlen and her children. Yes, I know. But who are they?"

Sally stepped away from the stove and came closer to me.

"Henry, your father will explain that to you. Just go out there and get to know them. Dinner will be ready in a few minutes." Sally took me by the shoulders and turned me toward the door. I went back to the living room and found my father sitting on the couch with Mrs. Von Ohlen. Sarah was sitting between them, and Roger was sitting in the chair where my father usually sat.

"Dinner will be ready shortly," I said. After I spoke, I realized I had interrupted a conversation my father was having with Mrs. Van Ohlen and her children. They all looked at me like I had three heads.

"Thank you, Henry," Father said.

When dinner was ready, Sally called us into the dining room.

"Margaret, why don't you sit right here." My father pointed to the chair next to him on his right and pulled it out for her. "Sarah, you can sit there next to your mother."

He then pointed to the chair next to him on the left, the chair I usually sat in. "Roger, you sit here."

I had been walking to my chair and stopped when my father told Roger to sit in it. I looked at my father, wondering where I was supposed to sit.

"Henry, you can sit there at the end." He pointed to the end of the table opposite his seat.

I sat where I was told, feeling out of place.

Sally served our meals. We had roast pork with mashed potatoes and green beans. When Sally walked behind me, she patted me on the back.

My father dominated the conversation, talking about the house, the neighborhood, the area schools, and our large backyard. It sounded like someone who was trying to sell a house rather than hold a dinner conversation.

I ate my dinner and let the others talk. Unless I was asked a direct question, I stayed quiet. The whole evening felt strange, and I didn't want to do or say anything that might prolong it.

Sally cleared the plates from the table and said that dessert would be ready in just a few minutes.

"I suppose now is as good a time as any to tell you all why we got together tonight," my father said. He looked at Mrs. Van Ohlen and smiled, then turned his attention back to the table. "Margaret and I have decided to get married. The wedding is in two weeks."

Mrs. Van Ohlen hugged Sarah, who didn't seem to understand what my father had just said.

"Congratulations, Mother," Roger said. "You too, Mr. Ross."

"Thank you, Roger."

I stared at my father, unable to speak. Were these people—people I had just met—going to be moving into our house?

"Henry, is there anything you'd like to say?" my father asked.

"Married?" I had not intended it, but my voice was filled with disdain. "That's wonderful. Congratulations." I tried to recover, but my voice was flat, revealing how I truly felt about my father's news.

Chapter 4
(1917)

The house was sweltering in the summer heat. We had electric fans set up all over the house, but they just blew hot air around, providing precious little relief from the thick, humid air. This was the type of day my mother would have wanted to spend at the beach, enjoying the breeze off the lake. I had not been back to the beach since she and Philip drowned. Too many bad memories.

I went out to the backyard in hopes of cooling down. We had a large oak tree in the backyard that provided shade. A gentle breeze blew the leaves, causing a constant rustling sound and providing a welcome, albeit small, reprieve from the heat.

I sat on one of the swings that hung from the big oak. My father hung two swings from the tree after Margaret, Roger, and Sarah moved into our house. He had never hung a swing for Philip and me.

I had only been outside for about five minutes when Sarah joined me. She sat on the other swing and began moving back and forth. After a minute or two, she stopped and turned her attention to me.

"Why do you hate Roger?" she asked.

In the two years I had known her, Sarah had gone from a shy ten-year-old to a chatty twelve-year-old who was quick to speak her mind. If she had a thought, she spoke it. I appreciated that about her. Unlike Margaret and Roger, who were both restrained and diplomatic, constantly leaving me wondering exactly what they were saying, I always knew what was on Sarah's mind.

"I don't hate Roger," I said. "Why would you think that?"

"You don't treat him very nicely," she said.

"Did he tell you that?"

Sarah began swinging slowly back and forth. The rope that tied the swing to the big branch overhead creaked as she swung. "No, my mother did. She said that Roger looks up to you, but you don't give him the time of day."

I knew exactly what Sarah was saying. It was true. I didn't have any use for Roger, but I couldn't admit why to anyone without sounding like a petty louse. At school, I got As and Bs. Roger got all As. I was a good athlete, but Roger was better. Maybe even better than Philip had been. In fact, he had recently started rowing for the Lincoln Park Boat Club, something few rowers in the area were good enough to do. Worst of all, Father made the time to watch Roger compete, something he had never done for Philip or me.

"That doesn't mean that I hate him." It was a weak retort, but it was the best I could do.

Sarah swung back and forth slowly. She stared up into the tree.

"We like living here," she said. "When daddy was killed in the car accident, we had to move out of our house and moved in with my grandparents in Evanston. But there wasn't room for all of us. We like it better here."

I grunted. Was that why Margaret married my father, because he had a big house? I wanted to tell Sarah that she and her brother and mother were not welcome at our house, but I knew that wasn't true. I was the only one that disliked having them there. My father was happier than I had ever seen him, and Sally loved having more people to cook for. She got along especially well with Margaret. It was like everyone but me had forgotten about my mother and Philip.

"Do you like having us here?" Sarah asked.

I didn't want to have this conversation with Sarah. I stood.

"I have to go in the house," I said. I preferred dealing with the sweltering heat inside than with Sarah's questions outside.

Chapter 5
(1918)

The high school gym had been decorated with colorful streamers and paper lanterns for the graduation ceremony. When it was over, I turned my cap and gown in to Mrs. Olson, the teacher in charge of the graduation committee, and I met my father in the lobby.

"Where's everyone else?" I asked. My father had been accompanied by Margaret, Roger, and Sarah, but they were not with him now.

"I had them wait for me in the car," he said. "I wanted to talk to you."

I wracked my brain to think of the last time my father and I had engaged in an extended conversation. Since marrying Margaret, he had gotten into the habit of relaying messages to me through her.

"What do you want to talk about?" I asked.

Father looked around the lobby, then motioned me to follow him. We walked past the gym doors, then down the corridor that led toward the classrooms. Around the corner from the gym, near the cafeteria, he found a bench away from the graduation crowd and motioned for me to sit. I thought he would sit too, but he didn't.

"I wanted to tell you that I'm proud of you for graduating," he said. "An education is an important thing, and I'm looking forward to you going to the University of Chicago next year."

"I'm excited about that too," I said.

My father paced back and forth in front of me, his hands clasped behind his back. He stared at the floor as he paced.

"I think you should get a jumpstart on college and find yourself an apartment in Hyde Park, near the school."

"I thought I was going to live at home." We had talked about this previously and the plan was for me to live at home and commute to college.

"I think it would be better if you lived on your own." He continued to look down at the floor. "You need to learn to be more independent."

The conversation did not make sense to me. We had gone over all of this before. It was his idea to have me live at home to save money on room and board.

"But we talked about this," I said. "We agreed that…"

"I know, but I've been giving it some thought, and I think it would be best for you to live on your own, in your own apartment. Of course, I'll pay for your living expenses as well as tuition."

"My own apartment?"

"Yes. In fact, I think it best if you look for a place right away. It will give you a chance to get used to the neighborhood before classes start." My father nodded as he paced, as if trying to convince himself of what he was proposing.

"I just thought I was going to…"

Father stopped pacing and stared at me. His voice rose and he gestured with his hands. "Henry, I can't…I have a second chance. Do you understand? I have a second chance to be happy. A second chance with a family. But with you in the house, all I see is your mother and brother, and what happened…" His voice trailed off. He took a deep breath and exhaled loudly.

"I think it would be good for you, Henry." His voice was now calmer. "You should learn to live on your own. This is a good opportunity for you."

"You want me out of the house?" Tears welled up in my eyes.

"It's for the best," he said. "You'll have your own place."

He was trying to sell me on the idea, as if it was all for my benefit, but he had let his mask slip. This wasn't about me. It was about him and his new family. Tears rolled down my cheeks and I wiped them away. I willed myself to stop crying. I refused to give him the satisfaction. I stood from the bench and cleared my throat.

"I'll start looking for an apartment right away."

"I think it's for the best," he said. "Let's go home."

He motioned for me to join him, but I took a step in the opposite direction.

"I'm going to walk home." Before he could object, I walked away.

Chapter 6
(1918)

My father had instructed me to major in either economics or finance, but when I registered for classes, I registered as a music major with an emphasis on piano. The music department was small and became my second home. If my father knew I had gone against his wishes, he never mentioned it.

I was working three different part-time jobs while going to school full-time. I studied for classes late in the evenings and on Sunday, my only day off work. Although my father was paying for me to go to college, including the cost of my apartment, I was working hard to save up money for after school. I had decided that once I graduated, I didn't want to have anything to do with my father or his money.

The phone rang one Sunday morning. I had just gotten out of bed and was feeling groggy. It was Margaret.

"How are you, Henry," she asked. "We haven't heard from you in some time."

What she said was true. I had made no effort to talk to her or my father since moving out of the house. I did not miss seeing any of them, although I felt bad that my feud with my father also meant I no longer saw Sally.

"I'm fine." I felt no compunction to explain my estrangement.

"Well, I was hoping you could come home next week to spend Thanksgiving with your family."

That was not my home. They were not my family. "I'm sorry, Margaret. I'm tied up with work and studying. I won't be able to make it."

I don't think she expected to be turned down.

"Oh, are you sure? We'd all love to see you."

"Unfortunately, I just don't have time."

There was a pause. "I know your father will be disappointed, as will I," she said. "Roger and Sarah—well, all of us—miss seeing you."

"I have to run," I said, not wanting to prolong the conversation. "But thanks for calling."

The same thing happened at Christmas. They invited me. I declined. That chapter of my life was over. There was no point in revisiting it.

Chapter 7
(1920)

My time at University of Chicago went by in a blur. I was constantly on the go, taking classes throughout the year, including during the summer, and working various jobs. I had no time for a social life. The result was that I was exhausted and bored, but I had completed my degree and put together a nice nest egg for my post-graduation life.

I knew that my father and Margaret would insist on attending my college graduation, so I notified the school that I would not be attending graduation ceremonies. To their credit, my father and Margaret continued to invite me home for holidays and breaks, and I continued to decline their invitations.

As graduation neared, I sold most of my furniture and other possessions in preparation for my post-college life. I pared my life down to just two bags, and almost all of that was clothes. I was packing the few items that remained when someone knocked on my apartment door. I opened it to find a man in a suit and tie.

"Can I help you," I asked.

"I'm G. Earl Corbin," he said. "Are you Henry Ross?"

I told him I was.

G. Earl looked like a kid dressed up in his father's suit and tie. He was short with a baby face, and his suit was too big for him.

"I'm an attorney at Holden, Goldstein, and Richmond," he said.

I recognized the name of the law firm. It was the firm my father used.

"Your father has set up a trust fund for you, and he has asked us to administer it. I just need to get you to sign some papers so you can have access to the funds."

I had not expected anything like this from my father. I had avoided and rejected him since leaving home, not wanting to have anything to do with him. He had exiled me from my home so he could move on with his life. I had become an inconvenience to him, and I did not want nor need his money.

"I don't want it." I stood in the doorway and the attorney stood in the hallway.

"I'm sorry. What?" His eyes narrowed in a confused look. "It's free money."

"I understand what it is," I said. "I just don't want it."

He adjusted his glasses. "Can I come in?"

I hesitated. I really didn't want to discuss this, but I knew he was just doing his job. I felt kind of sorry for him.

I invited him in, and we sat at the kitchen table, one of the few remaining pieces of furniture left in the apartment.

The young attorney looked around the empty apartment and his eyes landed on my suitcases.

"Are you going on a trip?" he asked.

"I'm moving," I said.

He nodded his head. "Henry…Do you mind if I call you Henry?"

"Sure." I sat back in my chair.

"I just want to make sure you understand why I'm here."

I nodded, indicating he should continue.

"Your father set aside some money for you. He put it into a trust fund, and he wants you to use it to get your post-college life started."

He looked for some indication that I understood what he was saying.

"Okay," I said.

"It's free money," he said. "There's no obligations, no strings attached. You can do whatever you want with the money. If you don't want it for yourself, you can give it to charity or to a stranger on the street."

The idea of giving my father's money to someone he wouldn't approve of drew my interest, but I'd still have to accept the money from him, which was something I didn't want to do.

"I understand all of that," I said. "But I don't want it, and I don't want to give it away."

He took off his glasses and pulled a handkerchief out of his back pocket. He fogged the glasses with his breath, then cleaned them with the handkerchief. He put the glasses back on and pushed them up the bridge of his nose.

He chuckled. "I didn't know turning down a trust fund was something one could do." He tapped his fingers on the table and smiled nervously.

"I don't want to discuss the details," I said. "But there's a lot of history between my father and me, and I don't want his money."

"I see," he said.

We sat in silence. As we did, I thought about how much more comfortable my life would be having access to more money. In just a few days, I was leaving for France. All the arrangements had been made. The trip to New York by train, the ocean liner to Europe, and the apartment in Paris had cost me the majority of my savings. I intended to get a job once I got to Paris, but my father's money could make the transition less stressful. It would allow me to be more selective about the job I got. Even so, it wasn't worth it.

"I understand you have a job to do, but I simply don't want the money."

"Even to give it away?" he asked.

"Nope."

"Don't you at least want to know how much it is?"

"I don't."

He pulled out his handkerchief again and wiped sweat from his brow. "I'm just trying to think of how I'm going to explain this back at the office."

"Simple. Explain that I didn't want it."

"No one will believe me."

"Your fellow attorneys might not believe you, but I suspect my father will."

He put the paperwork back into his briefcase, stood, and offered his hand.

"Good luck to you, Mr. Ross. I hope you don't regret this."

Someday, I might wish I had the money, but I knew I would never regret turning it down.

Section 2

Paris
(1920-1921)

Chapter 8
(1920)

I stood in front of the apartment building on Rue Cardinal Lemoine in Paris and felt a wave of excitement course through me.

The apartment building stood six stories tall and made an impressive shadow on the street in the mid-day sun. From a distance, it looked clean and welcoming. Up close, it was worn and in need of repair. I had rented one of the cheapest apartments available, not wanting to burn through my savings too quickly.

The excitement I felt out in the street subsided when I went inside the building. The common area was crumbling and smelled of garlic and human waste.

I found the landlord, Monsieur Theriault, in his apartment. He seemed irritated by my intrusion until he finally recognized my name. "Yes, yes. Monsieur Ross. Welcome. I will show you the apartment."

The sound of our footsteps echoed throughout the stairway. We made our way to the fifth floor and Monsieur Theriault unlocked the apartment door. He held it open and motioned me in.

There was not much to the tiny studio apartment. A bed frame with a thin, stained mattress stood against one wall, a straight-back chair against another. I opened a closet door and found a bucket that served as a toilet. There was no kitchen or running water.

"This is very nice, no?" Monsieur Theriault asked.

I forced a smile and nodded.

"Bien. Bien," the old man said, holding his hand out as if asking for a tip.

I looked at his hand, then up at him. "Merci," I said, using my extremely limited French. "I think I'd like to lie down for a bit. It's been a very long day."

Monsieur Theriault dropped his hand and walked out of the apartment without saying a word.

I sat on the bed. The worn mattress sagged in the middle and the bed frame squeaked loudly when I moved. The trip had been long. From Chicago to Paris—first by train, then ship, then car, then ferry, then car again—I had been traveling for just over three weeks. I'd come all this way to end up in a dump. I assured myself that this was just temporary. I was looking forward to getting a little rest, then going out to find a job.

I fell asleep on the thin mattress and awoke with the sun the next morning. The dread I felt the night before had subsided a little, and I set out to find work.

My first full day in Paris dawned sunny and warm. I applied for jobs at Caisse d'Epargne and Banque de France. They were both hiring, they were impressed with my college degree, but neither of them could use an employee who could not speak French.

The next day, I got the same response from Crédit Foncier de France and Monnaie de Paris. On the third day, Librairie Jousseaume turned me down, telling me how impressed they were with my credentials, but they unfortunately could not hire an employee who only spoke English. They wished me luck and sent me on my way.

I fought the urge to be depressed. I started to realize that while making the decision to live in Paris, I had never considered the possibility that Paris had no use for me. I was an American—a non-French speaking American—who had little to offer. Despite my best efforts, the depression set in.

The afternoon of the third day, I called off the job search temporarily and went to Les Deux Magots, a small bistro near my apartment. I had eaten precious little the previous three days, and I desperately needed food in my stomach. Despite my hunger, I couldn't make myself order a full meal. I had to preserve what little money I had.

I ordered a single croissant and a glass of house Bordeaux. The waiter, a short man with thin hair plastered to his scalp, brought the croissant and glass of wine, and set them in front of me.

"Merci," I said.

"De Rein," the waiter said.

"May I ask you a question? Are you hiring?"

The waiter smiled but looked confused.

"Do you have any job openings?"

"Pardon moi. My English not so good." The waiter held up his hands in apology.

I shook my head. "Never mind. Merci beaucoup."

The waiter bowed and quickly walked away.

A man sitting a couple of tables away scooted his chair back and turned toward me. "Are you looking for a job?" The man spoke English with what I took to be a New York accent.

"I am, but I'm afraid I'm having some trouble."

"Where are you from?"

"Indiana originally, but I've lived most of my life in Chicago. I just graduated from university there."

"A college man," he said. "Can you write?"

The question caught me by surprise. "Sure, I can write."

The man wiped his mouth with his napkin and walked toward my table. "My name's Miles Bergeron. I'm the editor of the Paris Herald, the local English language newspaper. Would you like to write for a newspaper?" He spoke quickly, clipping his words.

Writing for a newspaper was not something I had really thought about, but considering I needed money, and a lack of French would not stop me from getting the job, I said I would be interested.

"Can you start tomorrow?"

"Tomorrow? Sure."

"Good, because we're short on bodies, and there's a lot of work to do."

I stood and excitedly shook Miles' hand. "Thank you," I said. "I'm looking forward to getting started."

"I'm happy to have you." Miles pointed at my croissant. "Maybe you'll even make enough money to buy a proper meal."

Chapter 9
(1920)

After two paychecks from the Herald, I could not wait any longer. I found a new apartment on Rue Saint Jacques with a bedroom, a nice living room, a small kitchen, and even a bathroom with running water. It was the type of place I had dreamed of when I decided to move to Paris.

Best of all, it was just around the corner from Brassier Balzer, one of my favorite restaurants. One night after work, I wandered over for dinner and a few drinks. Feeling a bit lonely, I wanted to be amongst people.

"Good evening, Pierre," I said to the maître d'.

"Bonsoir, sir. How are you this evening?"

"Peaches, Pierre. Just peaches."

Before Pierre could reply, a man approached and put his hand on my arm. "Sorry to interrupt, but I couldn't help noticing you're American.

"Yes, I am."

The man held out his hand. "I'm Cam Hawley from Philadelphia."

"Henry Ross from Chicago."

"I thought I recognized that accent," he said. "I'm with a group of other Americans. Would you like to join us?"

The thought of meeting other Americans here in Paris excited me. "Yes, that's very kind of you."

"Pierre, could you have another chair brought to our table?" Cam asked.

"Of course." Pierre motioned to one of his waiters.

At the table, ten or twelve people were busy talking and laughing, and didn't pay any attention to us as we approached.

"Everyone," Cam said, waiting for his friends to pay attention to him. "I found another American. I want you to meet…" He looked at me and smiled. "I'm sorry. I'm afraid I've already forgotten your name."

"Henry Ross."

"Of course. This is Henry Ross from Chicago." Cam went around the table introducing each person, which included Ernest Hemingway, James Joyce, Max Eastman, Gertrude Stein, and Sylvie Beach.

"It's nice to meet you all," I said.

A waiter brought a chair, and I squeezed in next to Cam.

"Where did you live in Chicago?" Ernest asked, his voice low and gruff.

"On the North side, near the lake."

"I escaped from Oak Park, not too far from you," Ernest said.

"Escaped?" I repeated and laughed. "Did you not like living there?"

"Oh, it's fine for the elderly and infirm. A little slow for me."

Several people laughed.

"You aren't by chance the Henry Ross I've been reading in the Herald, are you?" Cam asked.

"I am," I said, half proud and half worried I had written something he didn't like. "I recently became the jazz critic for the paper."

"Jazz critic? I thought that blowhard Ellis Winston was the jazz critic," Ernest said.

"He was, but he moved back to New York. I was already working for the paper, and since I play a little piano and follow jazz, I was asked to take over."

"Good riddance to Winston," Ernest said. "He couldn't hold his liquor and he was a hack writer. Paris is better off without him."

"Ernest, don't you think you're being too hard on the man?" Gertrude asked.

"Just the opposite," Ernest said. "I'm showing great restraint in my opinion. I wouldn't want our new friend to think me overly critical."

Everyone laughed.

"I'm not quite as critical of Winston as Ernest," Cam said, "but I can tell you that in the short time I've read your reviews, I have noticed an improvement."

"Thank you. That's kind of you to say."

A waiter came and Cam ordered two more bottles of wine and an extra glass for me. The drinks flowed freely as we discussed art, music, the

Great War, the joys of vermouth, the best wine to pair with fish, and great literature, which everyone seemed to have an opinion about, but no one could agree on.

"Some of us are meeting at Café de Medicis for dinner next week," Cam said. "Would you like to join us?"

"I would. Thank you, Cam." I thoroughly enjoyed the evening and the free-wheeling conversations with my new friends. For the first time in a long time, I felt stimulated. As I walked back to my apartment, I caught myself humming a tune, and I laughed, truly happy for the first time in Paris.

Chapter 10
(1920)

Since I arrived in Paris, I had heard stories about an American named Eugene Bullard. Supposedly, he was a fighter pilot in the Great War, had boxed all over Europe and North Africa, was a fabulous jazz drummer, and was running Le Grand Duc, one of Paris' most popular clubs. I couldn't believe all the rumors I was hearing, but I thought there might be a story about him I could write for the paper.

I went to Le Grand Duc for lunch on a cool, overcast day. Normally, whenever I had the chance, I preferred to sit outside at one of the sidewalk tables. But with the weather, I opted to sit inside. A tall, negro man showed me to my table. Although it was a Paris hot spot, it was my first visit to Le Grand Duc. The interior was dark with brass accents, and the air smelled of shallots, cooked meat, and cigarette smoke. The white tablecloths were clean and bright.

After the waiter took my order, I asked him about Eugene Bullard.

"Yes, monsieur. You have already met him."

"When?" I asked.

"He is the man who showed you to your table."

"No. No. That can't be," I said. "A negro showed me to my table." My confusion was obvious, and it made the waiter smile."

"Yes, that is Monsieur Bullard. Would you like me to introduce you to him?"

I hesitated, unsure what I was getting myself into. "Yes," I said. "I'd appreciate it."

A few moments later the waiter returned with the negro host. "Monsieur, I'd like to introduce Eugene Bullard."

Bullard extended his hand. "I understand you're a fellow American." His voice was deep and his accent southern.

"Henry Ross." I stood and shook his hand. "Um, from Chicago."

"Pleased to make your acquaintance, Mr. Ross. I'm from Georgia."

"Please, call me Henry." I felt odd. To that point in my life, I'm not sure if I had ever shaken the hand of a black man, and I'm certain I had never engaged one in a conversation. Sally was the only negro I had more than a passing acquaintance with. "Would you like to have a seat, Mr. Bullard?"

"Thank you. And please, call me Eugene." He sat and crossed his legs. His mannerisms were sophisticated and gentlemanly. He was unlike any negro man I had ever met. "What brings you to Paris?" he asked.

"I write for the Paris Herald."

"Of course." He leaned forward in his seat. "Henry Ross, the jazz critic."

"You've read my column?"

"I look forward to it," he said. "And you'll forgive me for saying so, but I enjoy your writing a great deal more than I did your predecessor."

"That's kind of you to say."

"What brings you to Le Grand Duc today?"

I took a drink of my wine. It was dry and quite good. "I wanted to meet you. I've heard incredible tales of your bravery and achievements."

"Ah, the stories," he said, smiling. "They are mostly exaggerated, I'm afraid."

Considering what I had heard, I assumed they must be, but I wanted to know for sure. I drank more wine. "I heard you flew a fighter plane in the war and received several medals for your bravery." My voice conveyed my skepticism.

Eugene sat back in his chair and recrossed his legs. "Oh, that's true. I flew for the Lafayette Flying Corp in the French Air Service. They gave me the nickname, the 'Black Swallow of Death.'"

"Really? What about the medals?"

"I received the Croix de Guerre, the Croix du combatant volontaire, and the Medaille de Verdun, along with a few others."

I nodded, surprised at what I was hearing. "What about boxing? I heard you were a boxer."

"Oh, that's true, too. Before the war. I was working as a jockey back in Georgia…"

"You were a jockey, too?"

Eugene laughed at my incredulousness. "For a short time. I had heard that negro men like me were treated better in Europe, so I left my job as a jockey, stowed away on a German freighter, and landed in Scotland. That's where I started boxing. I had a few fights in Scotland and England. I met Dixie Kid in London, and he agreed to train me. After a few more fights there, Dixie arranged for me to fight in Paris. That's how I ended up living here."

While Eugene spoke, I finished my wine. When he was done, I was staring at him, holding the empty glass. His story mesmerized me.

"Would you like another wine?" he asked.

I looked at the empty glass, then back at Eugene. "Yes, please."

Eugene motioned to the waiter and held up two fingers. "Did you hear anything else about me?"

"In fact, I did," I said. "I heard you also spent time as a jazz drummer. Is that one true, too?"

"I played with the house band at Zelli's for several years. Then I was asked to join a jazz group that played in Alexandria."

"Alexandria? In Egypt?"

The waiter brought a fresh glass of wine for each of us.

Eugene sipped his wine, then gently set the glass on the table. "Yes, in Egypt. I had a couple more fights while I was there, too."

"So, what part of these stories is exaggerated?" I asked. "It seems everything I've heard about you is true."

He took another sip of his wine. "I thought you may have heard that I can walk on water," he said. "That one's not true." Eugene smiled.

I burst out laughing. "You are quite a man, Eugene." I raised my glass and toasted him.

"Thank you, Henry," he said, returning the toast. "Can I ask you a favor?"

"Of course."

"Next week, an American-born jazz singer named Josephine Baker will be playing here at Le Grand Duc. She's extremely talented, and I'd like you to come see her and maybe write about her. Could you do that?"

"I'd be happy to," I said.

"I'll save you a table."

We shook hands and Eugene went back to work. I had never met anyone like him, so confident and accomplished, yet humble, gentle, and polite. I would have been taken by him even if he were white. But the fact that he was a black man and had accomplished so much had me in awe. It made me sad to think that if this man, even with everything he had accomplished in life, lived back in the United States, he would be looked down upon and disrespected. Maybe what Ernest had said not only applied to Oak Park, but to the entire country. It's fine for others, but not for me.

Chapter 11
(1920)

Café de Medicis was packed. I spotted Cam and his group at a large table in the front room and made my way through the crowd. A tall, thin woman with short dark hair stood near the bar. She was quite attractive, but it was her laugh that drew my attention. Her face lit up when she laughed.

"Henry, we saved you a seat," Cam called out, freeing me from my trance.

I turned my attention to Cam and the rest of the group.

"Bonjour, a tous," I said.

"Bonjour yourself," Ernest said. "You've got some catching up to do." He raised his glass and finished his wine.

"We were just discussing some of our favorite writers," Cam said.

"And Ernest was telling us why we were wrong to like them," Gertrude said. Everyone laughed. I had learned at my last meal with the group that most of them were writers of one sort or another. Cam was the European bureau chief for the Philadelphia Inquirer, and Ernest was a foreign correspondent for the Toronto Star. Writing and writers seemed to be their favorite topic of conversation.

The discussion continued, but my attention was on the laughing woman. She seemed to exude confidence in the way she gestured when she spoke. I couldn't help but watch her. Even while we ate, I tried to participate in the conversation, but my focus kept turning back to her.

"To me, his words aren't genuine. You can feel the insincerity coming up off the page," Ernest said. "Henry, do you know what I mean?"

I was oblivious to Ernest's words, caught in this woman's spell.

Ernest put his hand on my shoulder. "Rather than just staring, why don't you go over and ask her to marry you?"

I felt myself blush.

"You might as well," Cam said. "Or we could ask my wife to set you up with one of her friends."

Ernest laughed and shook his head. "I don't think you'd want that."

"Maybe later," I said. "I need to finish my meal." I cut a piece of my steak au poivre and put it in my mouth.

"Nonsense," Ernest said. "I'll introduce you." Ernest began to stand.

"No." I grabbed his arm and almost choked on my steak. "I'll take care of it."

Just then the woman stood and walked toward the bathrooms.

"Here's your chance," Ernest said.

Ernest's words caught me by surprise. "What? In the toilet?"

"No, you rube. On her way back."

Ernest nodded toward the bar. I looked at Cam for support.

"Might as well." Cam shrugged.

I pushed my chair back, stood, and went to the bar. I ordered a drink while I waited for the woman to return from the bathroom. When she appeared, I approached her. "Excuse me," I said. "I don't mean to be too forward, but I wanted to introduce myself. I'm Henry Ross." There was a moment of silence and I felt I had to fill it. "I'm the jazz critic for the Herald Tribune." The words just slipped out on their own.

"Do you also review plays?" She had a British accent.

"No, I don't."

"That's good, because I'm here in Paris as part of the production of The Dover Road, and I'm afraid it would be a conflict of interest to let you buy me a drink if you're going to review the show."

"Buy you a drink? Yes, of course. What are you drinking?"

"A Gin Ricky," she said.

I gave the bartender her order then turned back to her. When I did, she offered her hand.

"My name is Kimberly Kline." She paused a moment, then added, "I'm an actress." I couldn't help but laugh as I shook her hand.

She played the role of Anne in The Dover Road. Her company's first show was the following evening. Most importantly, I learned that she was single.

"How did you get into acting," I asked.

"I've been acting since I was a little girl. My parents had some contacts in the London theater community. I was just six years old when I was in my first play. I've been doing it ever since." She took a drink. "How did you get into newspaper writing?"

"A man at a restaurant offered me the job and I said yes."

"Do people often approach you at restaurants with job offers?"

"Not as often as you might think." She had a great laugh.

Kimberly finished her drink, and I asked if she would like another.

"I'm afraid we're leaving," she said. "We're meeting the rest of the company at The Ritz. Would you like to join us?"

"I would, but..." I looked over at my table.

Kimberly seemed to understand my dilemma. "The more the merrier."

We said our goodbyes and I returned to my table. I had left behind a half glass of wine when I went to meet Kimberly. I slurped it down and poured myself another.

"How did it go?" Ernest asked.

"She's lovely," I said.

"Did you ask her to marry you?"

"Not yet. She wants us to join her at The Ritz after dinner. Would you like to go?"

Everyone else seemed to have plans, but Cam and Ernest said they'd go.

"We need to see that you get married off," Ernest said. "We don't want to have to keep dragging you around town."

Chapter 12
(1920)

The evening was clear and cool, and we strolled through the dark streets of Paris like three drunkards, illuminated by the full moon. As we crossed the bridge over the Seine, Ernest stopped, unzipped, and let loose into the river below.

"I don't know what it is with him," Cam said, "but he loves to piss in public.

"I don't love it. I'm just often in public when I have to piss." Ernest bellowed a laugh.

When we reached The Ritz, Ernest and Cam found seats at the bar, and I went in search of Kimberly. She was at a table near the back, talking to two men and a woman. I tried to get her attention, and when I couldn't, I returned to Ernest and Cam.

"What are you doing back here?" Ernest asked.

"Kimberly is busy, so I thought I'd come back and get a drink."

"This place is too crowded," Ernest said. "If you really want to talk to this woman, you need to get her out of here."

"I couldn't agree more." I turned and Kimberly was standing right behind me. "Henry, why don't we go for a walk." She smiled and winked at my two friends.

"Yowza!" Cam said.

Ernest slapped me on the back. "She's a real bearcat," he said. "You two go enjoy the night. We'll just sit here and get bent."

Kimberly and I went out into the cool, moonlit night, walking slowly toward the river.

"Do you like being a writer?" she asked.

"I'm not really a writer," I said. "I mean, I write about jazz, but I know much more about music than writing. Cam and Ernest are real writers." I motioned back toward the bar. "Cam says that being a journalist is all he's ever wanted to do. Ernest hates it and is working on a book deal. He wants to write fiction."

"Are they good?" Kimberly asked.

"I'm not sure. I haven't read either of them."

"Maybe you should write a book."

"About what?" I asked. "I barely get by writing for the paper."

"Do you like your job?" Kimberly swayed when she walked, and we bumped our hips. I played it off like I hadn't noticed.

"It's odd. I never wanted to write for a newspaper. I sort of just fell into the job. Yet, it's pretty great. I go to jazz clubs around the city and write what I think about the performers. Instead of paying to go see greats like Louis Mitchell and the Jazz Kings, or Mabel Mercer, I get paid to see them. I almost feel like I'm cheating the newspaper."

"I feel the same way about acting," she said. "I love being on the stage. I almost think I'd do it for free if they didn't pay me."

"Almost," I said.

Kimberly laughed. "Almost."

"I'm going to see a new singer night-after-next by the name of Josephine Baker at Le Grand Duc. Would you like to join me?"

"I'm afraid I'm tied up every night for the rest of my time in Paris. I have the show."

Disappointment cratered in my gut.

"How about lunch," she asked.

"Lunch? That'd be swell."

Kimberly reached over and threaded her arm through mine. I was surprised at her forthrightness, but I wasn't complaining. I put my hand on her arm, and we continued our march toward the Seine.

Chapter 13
(1920)

When Kimberly arrived at Café de Medecis the next day for lunch, I was waiting with a bottle of wine and a big smile.

"Mr. Ross, how nice to see you." Kimberly curtseyed flamboyantly, which made me laugh.

"Wine for Mademoiselle?" I asked with a horrible French accent.

"Oui, oui. Merci," she said.

I poured her a glass of wine and a waiter came to take our lunch order. When he left, I made a toast.

"To *The Dover Road* and a successful run.

"I'll toast to that," she said.

After a glass of wine and some small talk, Kimberly asked me about my family.

"I think we should talk about that some time when things are gloomier and we're not having so much fun," I said.

My intention was to make sure my family's story did not interrupt our good time, but my answer seemed to pique her interest.

"Why do you say that? I want to know about your family now more than ever."

"Oh, it's just a sad story that I don't talk about much."

Kimberly sipped her wine. "You don't have to tell me. But I want to know."

The waiter came and took our lunch order. When he left Kimberly stared at me expectantly.

"Where were we? Oh yes, you were about to tell me about your family."

Kimberly's playfulness made me laugh. "The short version is my mother and brother both drowned when I was eight years old. My father couldn't be bothered to care for me, so I was raised by a negro woman named Sally. She became like a mother to me. She died last year."

"Oh, I'm sorry," she said. "What about your father?"

"He's still alive, last I checked. We don't speak."

"I'm sorry to hear that, Henry."

"Enough about my family. What about yours?"

"Not much happiness there either, I'm afraid. My father died five years ago. My mum was devasted by his death and killed herself a year later. That just leaves my brother and me, and I'm afraid we don't speak."

"Just two happy families," I said.

"Happy, indeed."

The waiter delivered our meals, and we began eating. I wanted to know more about Kimberly's family.

"Why don't you and your brother speak?"

"That's another gloomy story." Kimberly put her fork down and wiped her mouth with her napkin. "My father was quite successful. When he died, he left everything to Mum. When she died, the money was split between my brother and me. My brother, Malcolm—he's older than me—thought he deserved more than half the estate. I've never understood why he felt that way. Whatever the reason, he blamed me and hasn't spoken to me since my mum's funeral."

"Families are fun, aren't they?"

"Like a barrel of monkeys."

We finished our meals and drank the last of the wine. I asked Kimberly if she'd like another bottle.

"Better not. I want to be tip-top for the show tonight. Let's go for a walk."

We walked down the street to the Luxembourg Gardens. Near the Fountain of the Observatory, we found a patch of grass in the sun. I laid my suitcoat down for Kimberly to sit on.

"Do you ever miss your family?" she asked.

"I miss my mother and brother sometimes, but that was so long ago, I'm used to them being gone."

"What about your dad?"

"It feels like I lost him at the same time I lost my mother and brother. They died. He disappeared. He has a new wife and family now."

"I miss my parents," Kimberly said. "We were extremely close. They'd always come to my plays and made sure I was doing okay. I was angry at my mum for a time. I felt she had been a coward and had abandoned me."

"You don't feel that way now?"

"No, in a way I see what she did as romantic. She loved my father so completely that she simply couldn't live without him."

"I can see that."

"You can?" Kimberly asked.

I nodded, and Kimberly reached over, placing her hand on top of mine.

"I've enjoyed our time together, Henry," she said. "Thank you for inviting me."

"It's been swell. Thank you for saying yes."

"Perhaps we should do it again tomorrow," she said.

I stared at her and was amazed at her complete lack of self-consciousness. She was truly comfortable being herself and saying whatever was on her mind. I smiled. "I think that's a wonderful idea."

Chapter 14
(1920)

At Le Grand Duc, I was greeted by the maître d' and was taken to
a table at the front, near the stage. A bottle of champagne on ice—
compliments of the house—was waiting for me. Eugene Bullard knew how
to treat a jazz critic.

I had heard good things about Josephine Baker before I spoke to
Eugene—who said glowing things about her—but even that didn't fully
capture her energy and stage presence.

After a rousing first set, Josphine took a break. The house lights came
up and I saw Eugene across the room, making his way toward my table.
He had to stop every few steps to greet guests. When he finally made it, he
offered his hand.

"Henry, I'm so glad you could make it."

"I wouldn't have missed it," I said. I wanted to add, Afterall, it is my
job, but thought better of it. "Thank you for the champagne. Would you
like a glass?"

Eugene raised a cocktail glass he was holding. "No champagne for me.
Tonight is a diablo night."

"A diablo?" I asked.

"Lemon soda and cassis. Light and very refreshing."

"Sounds good."

"Are you enjoying the champagne?"

"Yes," I said. "It's wonderful."

"If you like champagne, I bet you'd like a French 75. It's what a lot of
the ex-pats are drinking."

I had not heard of the drink before. "What is it."

"It's a mixture of gin, champagne, and lemon. Tastes as good as champagne, but with a bit more kick."

"I'll have to try that. But for tonight, I'm enjoying the champagne."

"What did you think of our girl, Josephine?" he asked.

"I think she's wonderful. She's quite the performer."

"I trust she'll be getting a positive review from Paris' favorite jazz critic."

"I don't know what Paris' favorite jazz critic will say about her, but she'll certainly get a positive review from me."

Eugene laughed. "I guess that will have to do." He stood. "If you need another bottle of bubbly, just let Anthony know." He pointed to one of the waiters. "Enjoy the rest of the show." With that, Eugene walked away to greet more guests.

I poured myself another glass of champagne and began thinking about Kimberly. I had only known her for a few days, but she seemed to sneak into my every thought. I wished she could have been here with me, sharing the bottle of champagne and enjoying Josephine Baker's show. We only had one more day together and then she would be gone. I wished there was a way to make time stand still.

Chapter 15
(1920)

After lunch on our final day together, Kimberly and I returned to Luxembourg Gardens. We walked lazily past the many statues and fountains, talking about Kimberly's show, Josephine Baker's performance, the weather in Paris versus London, and anything else we could think of to stretch our time together.

We stopped at the Medici Fountain and sat on one of the cement benches.

"Tonight is our final show," Kimberly said. "We leave for London in the morning."

I bowed my head. "I know, and I'm not looking forward to you leaving."

"Will you write to me after I'm gone?" Kimberly smiled a hopeful smile.

I wanted to take her in my arms and ask her to stay. I wanted to tell her that I loved her and never wanted to be apart from her. Instead, I said, "Of course, I'll write."

I walked Kimberly back to her hotel. We made plans to see each other before she left for London in the morning, then I spent a sleepless night thinking about what I'd like to say to her before she went back home. Truth was, there was nothing I could say. I would look foolish asking her to stay, to give up her home and life in London to move to Paris.

The next morning, I found Kimberly in front of her hotel waiting for me. She was packed and ready to leave.

"I've had a wonderful time with you, Henry." She smiled and seemed to be holding back tears. The strong, outgoing woman I had come to know over the past few days suddenly seemed fragile. "Don't forget, you said you'd write."

Here was my chance. I could sweep her up in my arms, tell her I loved her, and we could start our life together. I nodded. "I won't forget."

"It's time to go, Kimberly," one of her castmates called out.

Kimberly looked over her shoulder at the bus and then back at me. "I have to go."

I nodded again, afraid I might cry.

Kimberly threw her arms around my neck and hugged me tight. I returned the hug and did not want to let her go. When we released each other, tears were streaming down her face. "Goodbye, my love." She put her hand on my cheek and gently kissed me.

I reached for her but was too late. She had turned and was getting on the bus. I stood, alone on the sidewalk, watching the bus drive away.

I walked back to my apartment, oblivious to the people on the street or the misting rain. I should have done more, said more. But what could I have said or done that would have made a difference? Kimberly lived in England, I lived in France, and nothing I could do was going to alter those facts.

For the next two months, I wrote to Kimberly almost every day. Although I saw Cam and Ernest once or twice during those two months, I was poor company. I was preoccupied with thoughts of Kimberly, and neither the drinks nor the conversation could pull me out of my funk.

"You're in love, aren't you, sport?" Ernest asked one night over cocktails.

"We should have warned him," Cam said. "It's not for the faint of heart."

I was soon to be alone in Paris. Ernest and his wife, Hadley, were going on holiday in Spain. Cam had been called back to Philadelphia. I stopped in to see Eugene once or twice but didn't want to burden him with my relationship problems.

About two months after she left, I was writing to Kimberly about how things were going at the newspaper, the rainy weather Paris was experiencing, an especially good meal I had at Café de Flore on Boulevard Saint-Germain. I read back over the letter and became frustrated. I was sharing everything with Kimberly but what mattered most. I wadded up the letter and threw it across the room.

I took out another piece of paper and stared at it for a moment. I wanted to tell Kimberly how I missed her terribly and longed to see her again. Even so, I didn't want to scare her away or have her think me a mad man. So, I kept it simple. I told her that I wanted to come for a visit to London and asked if she'd be willing to show me around. Then I waited for a reply.

When I received it, I was giddy with excitement. Kimberly said that she would adore seeing me and that she would be the best tour guide in London. She ended her letter with "How soon can you get here?"

Chapter 16
(1921)

Kimberly's flat was in a fashionable building near St. James Square. The common area on the first floor was ornate, with marble floors and a uniformed doorman at the front desk. When I told him I was there to see Kimberly, he smiled knowingly. "Oh, yes sir. She's waiting for you. You can go up to the third floor." The doorman motioned to the elevator.

Kimberly opened the door and was even more beautiful than I remembered. She wore a white, sleeveless champagne dress with fringe that went down below her knees, and a sequined band around her head. Her hug was stiff and formal, but I held that hug until Kimberly pulled away.

"Henry, it's so good to see you," she said.

"Hello, Kimberly." Something didn't feel right. Kimberly was too formal, not like the outgoing woman I remembered.

She invited me into her flat, and we both sat on the small loveseat in her parlor.

"Did you get settled into the Claridge?" she asked.

"Yes, it's a lovely hotel," I said. "It's very popular. I was lucky to get a room."

Kimberly stood suddenly. "Can I get you a drink?"

"No, thank you." I could have used a drink, but I didn't want Kimberly to walk away.

She sat again, putting her hands in her lap. "How was your trip?"

"It was swell." I smiled, trying to lighten the mood. "No problems at all."

"That's good." Kimberly reached for a small throw pillow, held it for a moment, then put it back where it had been. She rubbed the arm of the loveseat, seeming not to know what to do with her hands.

I cleared my throat and Kimberly leaned forward to hear what I was about to say. Unfortunately, I had nothing to say. The silence between us became awkward.

"Maybe we should go to dinner," Kimberly said. "I thought we could go to Wilton's. It's a lovely place, and it's not very far away."

"That sounds fine." Now I was being too formal.

Kimberly smiled uncomfortably, then led the way out of her flat.

At Wilton's, we were shown to our table, and Kimberly ordered a bottle of red Bordeaux. The waiter recognized her and said, "Very good, Miss Kline," then walked away.

I ran my hand along the edge of the table, trying to think of something to say. "This is a nice place."

"They specialize in seafood. Do you like oysters?"

"I'm not a big fan." I scrunched my face. "I thought I might try the fish."

Kimberly smiled politely and nodded.

"What do you think you might get?" I asked.

She studied the menu. "Maybe oysters or lobster. I'm not sure yet."

Now it was my turn to smile and nod. Our silence was interrupted when the waiter brought the wine.

I raised my glass in salute. I thought about toasting Kimberly's beauty or our reunion, but I couldn't push out the words. Instead, I said, "To our time in London." I stumbled over the words. We drank, then set our glasses on the table.

I had come all the way from Paris to sweep this beauty off her feet. I desperately wanted to open up to her, to let her know how good it was to see her again and how I had missed her. But I suddenly could not speak.

After the waiter took our dinner order, I steeled myself to say what I was longing to say. But Kimberly spoke first.

"Henry, is everything okay?"

"Yes, of course," I said from habit, then regrouped. This was my moment. No more holding back. "I mean, no. Things are not okay."

I took a deep breath. "I've missed you terribly, Kimberly. You're all I think about all day long, and it has been that way since the night we met at

Café de Medicis. I'm tired of being nice and following propriety. The truth is, I love you, Kimberly."

I sat back and exhaled. I was sweating from the effort and feared I had said it too loudly. I looked around, but no one seemed to have taken notice. I drained my wine glass.

Kimberly laughed, and quickly raised her hand to cover her mouth. "I'm sorry, Love, but that was wonderful. I had planned on saying the same thing to you."

"Really?"

"I had hoped to be more reserved and dignified—after all, I am British—but I think I like the way you said it even better." Kimberly laughed again, reaching across the table to take my hand. "Welcome to London, Love."

Section 3

England
(1921-1945)

Chapter 17
(1921)

We spent our honeymoon at the country estate of Kimberly's friend, the stage actress Sylvie Taylor, two hours outside of London. Sylvie told Kimberly that we should spend as much time there as we wanted, since she and her husband rarely ever visited.

We wandered from room to room in the big house, spending most of our time in the library, drinking wine in the garden, or lazing in the bedroom. The time alone together was good for both of us. We reveled in the quiet and solitude.

We spent afternoons in bed, napping and making love. One afternoon, after I woke, I watched Kimberly sleep. The sun angled sharply through the window and spilled onto the bed. When she woke, she gave me a sleepy smile.

"Hello, Love," she said.

"Hello yourself."

"Are you spying on me whilst I sleep?"

"That and doing some thinking."

"Oh, really? About what?"

"When we get back to London, I'll need to get a job. I have a wife to support now. I can't be a lollygagger."

"We're not going back to London," Kimberly said. "We're going to stay here for the rest of our lives and let Sylvie pay the bills."

I laughed. "If that's copacetic with Sylvie, I'll go along with it. But if not, we'll need another plan."

Kimberly shifted from her prone position and leaned up to kiss me. She held my face in her hands for a moment, then lay on her side, the two of us mirrored images of one another. "What is it that you'd like to do?"

"I could try to get a job with one of the newspapers," I said. "I have some experience, and I think Miles would give me a good recommendation."

"You could, but it doesn't sound like that's what you want to do."

"I enjoyed writing for the newspaper, covering jazz, but I'm not really a writer. What I'd really like to do is own a jazz club like the ones in Paris. I did some checking, and there aren't any clubs like that yet in our area."

"Then that's what you should do," she said.

"You wouldn't mind?"

"Why would I mind? I want to see you happy."

I rolled onto my back and stretched my arms over my head. "It will be a lot of hours, especially in the beginning. And I'll be out late at night."

"At least I'll know where you are. I can come to see you when I get lonely."

"Maybe you can serve drinks?" I laughed at the notion of Kimberly working in a bar.

"I think I'd rather just walk around being the boss's wife. I don't actually want to work. I just want to look important."

I laughed. "You can't help but look important."

Kimberly reached for me, pulling me closer. "Come here," she said. "I have something important I'd like you to do." She pulled the sheets over our heads, blocking much of what remained of the late afternoon sun, submerging us into a dark, lusty twilight.

Chapter 18
(1921)

We named it The Blue Note, and the first band we hired was King Oliver's Creole Jazz Band out of New Orleans. The band, led by Trombonist Joe "King" Oliver, featured a young trumpet player by the name of Louis Armstrong.

During the week, I played piano, or hired a local to play, then two or three times a month we'd bring in a touring act like Coleman Hawkins, Duke Ellington, Paul Whiteman, or Django Reinhardt. Jazz was growing more popular, and Londoners were desperate to find a place that featured it. Even as other jazz clubs popped up, The Blue Note continued to do brisk business.

"You love this place, don't you?" Kimberly asked. We were at the bar one afternoon before the evening rush.

"It's been a lot of work, but I guess I do love it."

Kimberly was holding a cocktail napkin, and she began to tear it into small pieces. "I love seeing you happy," she said. "And I know the club makes you happy." She looked away and brought her hands to her face.

"What is it, Kimberly? What's wrong?" I put my hand on Kimberly's shoulder and turned her toward me.

"I don't want this to be bad news," she said. "Henry, I'm pregnant."

I jumped off the bar stool and embraced my wife. "Bad news? Kimberly, this is wonderful."

"Are you sure? Do you really think so?" She stopped crying and her eyes widened hopefully.

"Yes, of course." I took a napkin from a stack on the bar and wiped tears from her cheeks.

Kimberly took the napkin from me and dabbed her eyes. "You don't think it's too soon? The club's barely a year old."

"No, it's perfect. Everything's perfect."

I embraced Kimberly, then called to Jeffrey Coe, my assistant at The Blue Note.

"Jeffrey, something has come up and I'm going to have to leave. Can you handle the club tonight?"

"Sure, boss," Jeffrey said. "No problem."

"Good. I have to take my wife out to celebrate."

***

We went to Wilton's, the same restaurant we had gone to on my first night in London. I was over the moon, but Kimberly was not as happy as I thought she should be.

We held hands across the small round table. The white tablecloth was starched and rough against our skin.

"Is anything wrong," I asked.

"No." She smiled "What could be wrong? We're having a baby."

She said the right words, but they seemed to lack conviction. "It seems like you have something on your mind. Something you're not telling me?"

"There is something. I've been thinking, but I'm not sure. I don't know how you'll feel about a decision I want to make."

"Tell me what you're thinking, and we'll both find out how I feel about it." We both laughed.

"Good idea, as always." Kimberly pointed at me and winked, as if to say, Good on you. She took a sip of her wine, then took a deep breath. "When we have the baby, I don't want to work anymore. I want to stay home and be a mum."

"That's it?" I asked. "If that's what you want to do, I think it's wonderful."

"But you married a semi-successful actress, not a plain old house frau."

"No, I married a very successful actress," I gave Kimberly's hands a squeeze. "But being an actress isn't why I married you. You are a beautiful, intelligent, capable woman. I fell in love with you, not with an actress. And I'll continue to love you no matter if you are up on a stage or in the kitchen fixing my dinner like a good house frau."

Kimberly let out a loud laugh. "You do have a way with words," she said. "I know you don't want to rely on the money I got from my parents, but if the club doesn't make enough, we can always dip into it."

Kimberly and I had talked about living off the money she received when her parents died, but as her husband, I felt it was my duty to provide for her.

"Let's see what happens," I said. "No matter what, we'll be okay."

"Can you believe it?" She brought my hand to her mouth and kissed it. "We're having a baby."

Chapter 19
(1922)

We gave up our flat in London and moved to a two-story home in Osterley, about an hour outside the city. The London flat was close to The Blue Note, but Kimberly desperately wanted to raise our children in a less crowded and noisy environment.

The house was near the Indian Gymkhana Cricket Club, not too far from the A4. It gave us easy access to London but was far enough away from the city so we could have a large garden and a bit of privacy.

As soon as we moved in, Kimberly started arranging the house. I mostly took orders, painting the walls I was told to paint or moving furniture to where Kimberly wanted it. We took breaks in the garden to enjoy the late spring sun, and spent evenings on the couch, Kimberly's feet in my lap, listening to the BBC.

Pregnancy agreed with Kimberly. Even as her belly grew, she refused to slow down. She was determined to make our home perfect for the arrival of our son or daughter.

One evening we were on the couch listening to Dvorak's Cello Concerto. Per usual, Kimberly's feet were in my lap.

"I almost forgot to tell you," she said. "You received a letter from Chicago today. I think it's from your father." She reached over and plucked an envelope off the end table and handed it to me.

I stared at the envelope for a moment, not sure what I wanted to do with it. The return address was "Ross" and my old address in Chicago. I recognized the handwriting as my father's.

"How did he know our address?"

My question was rhetorical, but Kimberly had an answer.

"I sent your family a Christmas card last year," she said. "I hope you're not angry."

"My brow furrowed. "You sent them a Christmas card?" I was trying to make sense of what Kimberly had just told me. "Why?"

Her eyes darkened. "I'm sorry, Henry. I was sending Christmas cards and thought it would be nice to send one to your family. I didn't think it through." Tears welled up in her eyes.

I was confused. Kimberly knew how I felt about my father It made no sense to me. Even so, I didn't want to upset her.

"It's okay,' I said. "No harm. I'm just not interested in reading a letter from my father." I tossed the unopened envelope on the coffee table.

"You're not angry?" she asked.

I rubbed her feet. "No. You didn't mean to start anything."

Kimberly's shoulders relaxed and she let out a sigh.

We sat silently listening to the music. I closed my eyes, thinking about what my father might have said. Whatever it was, I didn't want to know about it.

I continued to rub Kimberly's feet when she let out a yelp, like a wounded dog. I thought I had hurt her.

"What's wrong?"

Kimberly grimaced and grabbed her belly. "I think I just had a contraction."

"Isn't it too early for that?" She was barely eight months pregnant.

"It is, but…" She grimaced again and arched her back. When the contraction passed, she slid her feet off my lap and onto the floor. She stood. "Maybe I just need to…" She yelped again and looked down at her legs. They were wet. "My water, Henry."

I grabbed the bag Kimberly had prepared a week earlier and helped her to the car. It was a cool, crisp night and the nearly full moon illuminated the driveway.

"I don't want to lose the baby," Kimberly said.

"You won't," I said. I was trying to be reassuring, but what did I know? I was not a very religious man, but I instinctively said a silent prayer that Kimberly and our baby would be safe and healthy.

***

We named him James Patrick Ross, but immediately called him Jimmy. He was a small baby who had all his fingers and toes. Kimberly took on the role of mother perfectly. She was loving and attentive to Jimmy, anticipating his need for a meal or a diaper change. I felt lost and helpless. Kimberly thought my helplessness was a hoot. She laughed when I tried to change Jimmy's diaper or feed him a bottle.

"Don't feel too bad, Love," she'd say. "You're merely a man."

Despite my helplessness, I loved being a father. I spent hours watching Jimmy sleep or crawl on the floor. It stirred in me a different kind of love; a parental love that I had heard about but didn't truly understand until Jimmy was born.

At eight months old, Jimmy still slept in a bassinet in our bedroom. We prepared a room for him across the hall from ours when we bought the house, but Kimberly wasn't ready yet to let him sleep that far away.

One night, Jimmy's crying woke me. I was going to get out of bed to tend to him, but Kimberly put her hand on my chest.

"He's hungry." She got out of bed, and I went back to sleep.

Sometime later, I awoke when Kimberly crawled back into bed. She slid across the mattress to my side and lay atop me. She kissed me gently, then whispered in my ear, "I want another baby."

Chapter 20
(1923)

I got into the habit of only spending a few days each week at the club. Truth was, Jeffrey was a better manager than me. I loved the music, but managing employees and ordering supplies was a headache. I preferred to stay in Osterley with my son and newly pregnant wife.

"If the club's not making enough, we can always dip into my money," Kimberly said.

"The club is doing fine," I said. "In fact, it seems to do better when I'm not there." We both laughed, even though what I said was true. Then I became more serious. "Plus, you know how I feel about using your money. It's my job to provide for our family."

Kimberly rubbed her expanding belly. "What's the point of having my parent's money if we never use it? There's no shame in taking advantage of our good fortune."

I had no answer. Dipping into Kimberly's money could make things easier. To be sure, there were times when money was tight. Even so, providing for our family was my responsibility.

We sat quietly while Jimmy did his best to walk around the room. He used the table as leverage to stand, then he'd take a step or two before collapsing to the ground. After a moment, he'd use the armchair to stand and do it all over again.

Kimberly adjusted herself on the couch and placed a pillow under her growing belly. It was difficult for her to see Jimmy fall to the ground. I often reminded her that he needed to do this on his own to gain strength and learn to walk. I wasn't telling her anything she didn't already know. Still, it was tough for her to stay uninvolved.

Kimberly wiggled herself off the couch. "I have to go to the loo," she said. "Can I bring you a drink on the way back?"

"No, thanks," I said.

Kimberly went upstairs to the bathroom. Jimmy maneuvered around the coffee table, then fell to the ground again and decided to stay there for a while. He sat cross legged on the floor and examined his bare foot.

Kimberly screamed.

I froze for a moment, stunned.

"Kimberly, is everything okay?"

"Henry, come quick. Oh, God."

Kimberly was on the bathroom floor. Blood dripped from her legs. "The baby." She sobbed. "I'm sorry, Henry."

There was a bloody mess in the toilet.

"We need to get you to hospital." I grabbed a couple of towels from the bathroom closet and wiped off Kimberly's legs. She took the towels from me.

"I'll do this," she said through her tears. "You get Jimmy. See if Nancy can watch him."

There was nothing the hospital could do. The baby was gone.

The doctor wanted to keep Kimberly overnight just to be safe. "I want to make sure that the bleeding has stopped completely," he said.

He gave Kimberly a sedative to help her sleep and she struggled to keep her eyes open. "Henry, there was so much blood."

"I know, Love." I took her hand. "You should try to get some rest."

"I want another baby." Her words were slurred, and her eyes were closed. Her hand went limp in mine. I placed it across her chest and kissed her forehead. "I love you, Kimberly," I said. "I'll be back tomorrow."

When I returned home, I made dinner for Jimmy, and he fell asleep in his playpen. I went upstairs to the bathroom where I mopped the floor and cleaned the outside of the toilet bowl. Then I stood and stared at the bloody mess that was left. Our baby. I knew I needed to flush the toilet but could not seem to do it.

I leaned against the sink, still staring. Was it a boy? A girl? I closed my eyes and rubbed my forehead. I tried fighting back tears but failed. Our baby.

I took a deep breath and wiped the tears away. "Oh, bloody hell." I reached for the pull chain. "I love you, little one." Then I pulled the chain.

Chapter 21
(1923)

I was sitting on the bed next to Kimberly when the doctor came into the room. Kimberly looked much better than she had the night before. I even got her to smile once or twice. The doctor asked how she felt.

"I'm doing well." She said in a matter-of-fact tone.

"That's good news," the doctor said. "I wanted to talk to you about the examination I did when you came in yesterday."

Kimberly sat up in bed. I helped her adjust the pillow behind her back.

"You have an abnormal growth in your uterus. They're called fibroids. That's likely why you miscarried," the doctor said.

"We want to have another baby." Kimberly reached for my hand.

"Getting pregnant with fibroids is not a good idea," he said. "First, it can be difficult to get pregnant. And if you do, the pregnancy can be risky, to both the baby and the mother."

"Can you get rid of them, the…"

"Fibroids," the doctor said. "The treatment I recommend is to have a hysterectomy. That involves removing the uterus and the fibroids together."

"I can't have a baby without a uterus."

"It's the safest course of action."

Kimberly slumped in the bed.

"Is there any other way?" I asked, already knowing the answer."

"The hysterectomy would be my suggestion. Not doing anything is too dangerous in my opinion."

Kimberly stared out the window. She tuned out the doctor and went off into her own little world.

I thanked the doctor, and he left. A nurse came into the room and encouraged Kimberly to make an appointment with the doctor for a pre-operation exam and to schedule the hysterectomy. Kimberly still stared out the window. I promised the nurse we would make the appointment.

The ride home was quiet. Kimberly stared straight ahead, silent. I wanted to start a conversation, to break her out of her shell, but I wasn't sure what to say. We were nearly home when she finally spoke.

"I want another baby."

"I do too," I said. "But I want you more."

We rode the rest of the way without speaking.

Chapter 22
(1924)

Physically, Kimberly recovered quickly from her hysterectomy. Mentally, she remained detached. Nothing I said seemed to help, so I took to not saying anything.

With Christmas a few weeks away, I suspected that Kimberly was going to be in for a tough stretch. There were times she was so despondent I was afraid she might hurt herself. That fear might have just been my imagination getting the best of me, but I didn't want to risk it.

A week or so before Christmas, we went to London to shop. I suggested it after several days of Kimberly lying on the couch, me in my chair, and neither of us talking.

We were in Selfridge's on Oxford Street, and I took Jimmy for a walk around the store. He was always a bundle of energy and didn't like to stay still, which is exactly how Kimberly liked to shop, slow, methodical, taking in each item before moving on.

When we returned, we found Kimberly in the aisle with the baby clothes. Her eyes were red, and tears rolled down her cheeks. She didn't notice us until Jimmy wrapped his arms around her legs.

"I'm hungry, Mum."

We had promised Jimmy lunch at Sweetings while we were in London. Jimmy had not forgotten a previous visit when he had a bowl of ice cream with chocolate syrup on top. Kimberly and I enjoyed Sweetings because of the seafood and the black velvets, a mixture of Guiness and champagne.

I pulled Jimmy away from Kimberly. "Mum still has some shopping to do, Jimbo" I said. "Maybe we should leave her be."

"Actually, I could use some lunch." Kimberly wiped the tears from her face. She composed herself, then took Jimmy's hand.

***

We finished our meals and Jimmy was feasting on his bowl of ice cream. The waiter brought two black velvets and sat them in front of Kimberly and me. I was about to have a drink when Kimberly stopped me.

"Wait a minute. I'd like to make a toast."

The outgoing Kimberly—the one who made toasts—had been missing for quite some time. I turned my attention to her.

"Sometimes, when you're so focused on what you don't have, you lose sight of what you do have. It's time I started focusing on the wonderful things and people I have in my life." She raised her glass, and I did the same.

"To what we have," I said. We each drank our black velvets. I wanted to talk about what Kimberly had just said, to encourage her, but she had realized something very important, and I feared that talking about it would somehow diminish it.

Kimberly smiled at me, and her smile conveyed so much. It was an apology, a confession, and a sign she was back. Maybe not fully back, but she was on her way.

Kimberly turned her attention to Jimmy. "How's that ice cream?"

Jimmy tried to speak, but his mouth was full.

"That's okay," she said. "Enjoy it before it melts."

Chapter 23
(1926)

Kimberly and I were on either side of a blanket she had spread out on the sand, with Jimmy in between us, playing with a toy. We had talked about going on holiday to Villefranche-sur-Mer, in the south of France. She had gone there with her parents several times in her early years, and she wanted to share it with Jimmy.

We spent the day at Plage des Marinieres, a beach in Villefranche-sur-Mer of which Kimberly had fond memories. It was high season, so the beach was crowded. Large boats drifted lazily offshore, and people splashed in the blue-green water. Behind us were homes painted every color of the rainbow, which gave the beach a bright, cheerful feel.

I, however, was not feeling cheerful. Our visit to Plage des Marinieres was my first time at a beach since my mother and brother drowned.

Jimmy played with a toy truck but would periodically look at the people on the beach and the water beyond. I wanted him to stay on the blanket, but after watching people run in and out of the water, he wanted to give it a try.

"I want to go swimming." He pointed at the water.

"Why don't you stay here and play on the blanket?" I asked.

A group of three children, maybe ten or twelve years old, went running by, laughing. That seemed to make Jimmy even more eager to get out into the water.

"I'll go with you, Jim," Kimberly said. She stood and took Jimmy's hand as they walked toward the water.

I felt a bolt of panic. They walked across the soft, coarse sand, and when they got to the water's edge, I jumped up from the blanket and ran toward them, calling Kimberly's name. She turned and saw me running quickly toward her.

"What's wrong, Henry?" I must have looked half-crazed.

I did my best to compose myself. "Nothing's wrong," I said, trying to catch my breath. "I just want to come with you."

Kimberly tilted her head, a look of concern on her face. But after a moment, she relaxed and smiled. "Okay. Come on."

Kimberly held one of Jimmy's hands. I took the other and we walked him into the warm, shallow water.

Jimmy sloshed around in water that only came up to his waist. Kimberly and I sat down, and Jimmy ran around us, splashing and giggling.

"When I was a little girl, my parents used to do this with me," Kimberly said. "I'd run around in the shallow water while my brother, Malcolm, sat up on a blanket and read a book. He refused to wear a bathing suit, instead sitting on the beach fully clothed in his shorts, button-down shirt, shoes, and socks. He was an odd child, so serious. He grew up to be a serious, odd adult.'

"It's strange that I've never met him," I said. "Afterall, he is your family."

"And I haven't met your father."

Kimberly was right. At our wedding, we had a couple of friends serve as witnesses, but we didn't invite anyone else. "Maybe it's best for both of us."

Kimberly laughed. "Maybe."

Jimmy continued to run circles around us. Every once in a while, he would trip and fall face first into the water, then stand up laughing.

Kimberly lay back, keeping her face above water. She stared into a cloudless sky. "This place brings back so many memories for me. My mum and dad were always happy here. They were so much more care-free than at home. I think maybe I was happiest here too." Then she caught herself. "I mean, until I met you." We both laughed.

It did my heart good to see Kimberly so relaxed and happy. The light was back in her eyes.

"I want to take you to see St. Michael's Church. And tomorrow, we should go to the market," Kimberly said. Her head was still tilted back, but her eyes were closed. "Oh, and there's a little restaurant near The Citadel, I can't remember the name, but we used to go all the time. I wonder if it's still open."

"We'll do whatever you like," I said. "I'm just along for the ride on your holiday."

Kimberly laughed. As she did, Jimmy jumped next to her, splashing water in her face. Kimberly sat up quickly and grabbed Jimmy, pretending like she was wrestling him. Jimmy screeched with glee.

Chapter 24
(1930)

Business at The Blue Note slowed. Our revenue dipped during the summer months, and by Christmas, the downturn worsened. An economic depression swept across the world. Although England had not been hit quite as hard as the United States, we were still feeling the effects.

But it was not just the depression that hurt us. Jeffrey was an astute businessman and did a great job with the employees, but he didn't know jazz. Our performance schedule became stale, with the same tired acts playing too often. We needed a big splash to put The Blue Note back at the forefront of the London jazz scene.

I reached out to my old friend, Eugene Bullard, in Paris. He was not only running Le Grand Duc, but had bought it outright from his friend, "Bricktop" Smith. As it had been for many years, life was good for Eugene Bullard.

I explained my situation and asked if he could put me in touch with Josephine Baker, who had played that wonderful show at Le Grand Duc all those years earlier.

"I'm not sure, my friend," Eugene said. "Josephine and I are not as close as we once were. She's being managed by an Italian cad named Guiseppi Abatino. He calls himself 'Count' Abatino, but I think he's a conman. Josey is sleeping with him and thinks he's the cat's meow. I doubt if he'll agree to have her play in London, but when she gets back, I'll talk to her and see what I can do."

"Gets back from where?"

"She's with Abatino doing shows in Yugoslavia. They're supposed to be back in Paris next week."

"I'd appreciate it if you could talk to her, Eugene. I really need to jumpstart things here."

Eugene promised he would talk to her. But when I still had not heard back a month later, I started work on a backup plan.

I had recently learned that the singer and actor, Paul Robeson, was living in London. He had been the only negro student at Rutgers University, where he played football. After graduation, he played in the National Football League, and simultaneously attended law school at Columbia University. But it was on Broadway where he really made a name for himself. Robeson starred in The Emperor Jones, and on the London stage in Show Boat. When time permitted, Robeson also did concerts, where he showed off his baritone-bass vocals.

I put out feelers, asking everyone if they had a connection to Robeson. To my surprise, the man himself called me one day at the club.

"I got a message that you were trying to reach me," he said.

"Indeed, I have been."

"Wait, are you American?" he asked.

"I am," I said. "But I've been living in England for nearly ten years. I married a local."

Robeson's laugh was deep and robust. "I live here too," he said. "But I brought my American wife with me."

After I proposed that he play a concert at The Blue Note, he put his wife, who was also his manager, on the phone. Ten minutes later we had a deal.

A few days later, Eugene called with news about Josephine Baker.

"She turned me down, Henry. She said she'd like to, but she knew that Abatino wouldn't let her. She said she was too tired from her trip to Yugoslavia to fight with him about it."

"That's a shame, Eugene. I know you…"

"Wait, there's more to the story." Eugene chuckled.

"Go on."

"I told Josey you'd be heartbroken because you weren't only a fan, but you'd written a glowing review of her when she first performed a Le Grand Duc. She remembered that review and said it was one of the best she had ever received. She promised to talk to Abatino about it, and she called yesterday to say if you have room on your schedule in February, she'll do it."

My head was spinning. When I told Eugene about Paul Robeson, he suggested we set them up to play on consecutive nights.

"If you want to make a splash, make a really big splash," he said.

The night of Robeson's show, I was nervous, but Robeson was a pro, and the show went off without a hitch. He sang jazz standards as well as numbers from the stage shows he had been in. The sell-out crowd loved his performance.

Josephine Baker's show was an even bigger success. It was standing room only and the crowd was raucous. Josephine played off the crowd's energy and put on a masterful show, receiving three standing ovations and doing two encores. She closed the show with her hit, "I Wonder Where My Baby is Tonight."

After the show, I went backstage to thank Josephine for playing The Blue Note. "I truly appreciate it."

"Thank you for asking," she said. "And thank you for your review of my show at Eugene's joint. I've never forgotten your kind words."

I was about to speak when Josephine's manager, 'Count' Abatino, interrupted. "Yes, we must go now. It's time for the payment, then we go."

Abatino spoke English, but with a thick Italian accent. His tone was abrupt and unfriendly. I had the payment for Josephine in cash and counted it out on a nearby table.

"Maybe an extra fifty pounds," Abatino said. "She do a good show."

"We had an agreement," I said. "You told me…"

"No, Guiseppe," Josephine said. "Henry's a friend and we had a deal."

Abatino looked at Josephine, then back at me, looking like he wanted to explode. He threw up his hands. "Ehhhh," he growled, and stomped out of the room.

I looked sheepishly at Josephine. I wasn't sure what to say.

"Thank you again, Henry," she said. "I'm sorry about that."

"I understand." I bowed toward Josephine and left the room.

Back in the barroom, the crowd was nearly all gone. Kimberly was sitting on a barstool talking to Jeffrey, who was cleaning behind the bar.

"Everything okay," Kimberly asked.

"Yeah, it's great. What a show, huh?"

"It was a great show. So, why do you look like you just lost your best friend?" Kimberly asked.

My brief run-in with Abatino had me reeling, but it wasn't something I wanted to talk about. "Do I? I don't know."

"Are you sure you're okay?" Kimberly asked.

I tried to look like everything was normal. "Yeah, I'm fine."

"Hmmm." Kimberly squeezed my hand. There was no hiding things from her.

Chapter 25
(1931)

Arms out like airplane wings, Jimmy ran around the garden shed seeing how fast he could go. Kimberly and I had cheered him on, but even after we stopped, he kept running.

After a few more rotations around the shed, I called him over to the patio. "Why do you like to run so much, Jimbo?"

"I like to go fast," he said.

I opened my mouth to say something else, but he was off, running behind the garden shed.

Kimberly laughed. "That boy is full of energy."

"That he is," I said. "I wish he'd share a little with me."

Jimmy was about to turn nine and rarely sat still. He was an athletic kid who played football in the Osterley Youth Football program and loved the competition.

Kimberly turned her chair so she could face me. "You got another letter from your father," she said. "I put it in the box, but I can get it if you want to read it."

Over the years, I had received several letters from my father, but I had not read any of them. I would have just as soon thrown them away, but Kimberly had saved them in a shoe box she kept in the hall closet. She said she did that in case I ever wanted to read the letters. I assured her that time would not come, but there was no harm in letting her save them.

"No. The box is where the letter belongs." I cleared my throat. "I think I'm going to go to the club this afternoon. It's been a week since I've been there, and I feel I should make an appearance."

"And maybe play a little piano?" Kimberly asked.

"I just might," I said. "I miss it."

"I know you do. Jimmy and I will be fine." Kimberly reached for my hand. "Enjoy yourself, but don't stay out too late. I don't like being alone in that big bed."

I did not take Kimberly's good mood for granted. Most of her days were like this, loving and present. But there was still the occasional day when dark clouds moved in, and she would spend the day napping or be by herself in the garden.

As much as I liked being home with her and Jimmy, I had a business to run and had been absent for too long.

The club was busy for a Tuesday night. Jeffrey was behind the bar, and he greeted me when I walked in.

"Who's that good looking stranger?" His gruff voice was loud enough so everyone in the bar could hear. "Don't tell me. You look familiar."

I walked to the bar and shook Jeffrey's hand. "How are you, Mr. Coe?"

"Full of piss and vinegar," he said. "How 'bout yourself?"

Jeffrey poured me a Guiness. "I'm doing good. I just missed this place and thought I might play a little bit tonight."

"We're happy to have you. Isn't that right, Paddy?" Paddy, the other bartender, had worked at the club almost as long as Jeffrey.

Paddy looked across the bar and stared for a moment. "I'm afraid I don't know that bloke, but it's good to have him here just the same."

"Nice to see you too, Paddy," I said.

Jeffrey laughed, then leaned across the bar. "How's the missus?" His question had a conspiratorial tone. I had confided in Jeffrey about Kimberly's struggles since losing the baby.

"She has good and bad days," I said. "But a lot more good days than before. I think she's doing okay."

"That's brilliant. Kimberly is a good woman."

"She is indeed."

I greeted a few other people, then sat down at the piano. It always amazed me how playing piano calmed me. Any stress or anxiety I was feeling seemed to melt away as soon as I put my hands on the keyboard. The piano was like a magic elixir, and I needed it now more than ever.

Chapter 26
(1936)

We gathered around the radio for the nightly Olympic broadcast. Even in England, people were abuzz about the performance of Jesse Owens, a black man from America, who had captured gold medals in the one hundred meters, two hundred meters, long jump, and the four-hundred-meter relay the previous week. And it all took place in Berlin, the heart of Germany, right in front of Adolf Hitler, a man who advocated for Aryan supremacy.

The gold medal performances by Owens made me think of Eugene Bullard. I wondered what he was up to these days. I had followed along with Ernest's writing journey, and I occasionally caught Cam's byline in the newspaper, but I hadn't spoken to Eugene in about five years. I wondered what had become of him. I assumed he still owned Le Grand Duc. Whatever he was doing, I wished him well.

Great Britain had high hopes for the eight-man rowing crew. We cheered for the home team, but I also had a rooting interest in the Americans. They were not expected to win a medal. In fact, it was a bit surprising they even made the finals, considering they were a bunch of young college students with relatively little rowing experience.

"The lads have to watch out for Germany." Jimmy sat on the floor in front of the radio, eager for the race to begin. "They're favored to win."

"Maybe the Brits need you on the rowing team, Jimbo. Maybe that would help them beat the Germans."

Jimmy laughed. "I don't think I'd be much help in a boat, but maybe on the pitch in 1940." Jimmy had grown into a strong, athletic kid, and he had talked about making the Olympic football team ever since he was a tot. Now, as a fifteen-year-old, he was just one, maybe two, Olympics away from giving that dream a try.

"Where are the next Olympics?" Kimberly asked, eyes on her knitting.

"In Japan," Jimmy said. "Are you going to come watch me there?"

"If you make the team." Kimberly looked at me and winked.

The rowing finals started. Jimmy turned the volume up. Great Britain got off to a good start, but so did Germany and Italy. The Americans fell back.

I watched Jimmy as the race unfolded. Each time the announcer mentioned the team from Great Britain, Jimmy sat up a little and pumped his fist. His beloved British footballers had gotten knocked out in the quarterfinals, losing to Poland. When they lost, I thought Jimmy might cry. He moped around the house the rest of the night. The next morning, I found him in the garden practicing his ball skills.

Germany led at the half-way point, with Italy and Great Britain battling for second place. The Americans had overcome a poor start and had moved into fourth place. The British crew made a surge, overtaking the crew from Italy, but the Italians responded, retaking second.

"Come on, lads. Come on." Jimmy sat up straight, legs crossed.

The effort to overtake Italy seemed to have spent the British crew. They fell back, overtaken by the Americans. The Brits fell back further, and Jimmy's shoulders slumped.

"Don't let the Germans win."

The announcers became excited. "The Brits have fallen off the pace, but the Americans have drawn even with the Italians. And they're both catching the Germans. As they near the finish line, all three boats are even. The crews are pushing, and as they cross the line it's…"

The announcer became silent, but the crowd roared in the background. Jimmy turned toward me. "Who won?"

I shrugged.

He turned back toward the radio. "Who won?" he pleaded.

The announcer cleared his throat. "We have a photo finish. To this reporter's eye, all three boats crossed the line at the same time. What I can tell you is Great Britain came home in fourth position, followed by Hungary and Switzerland. As for the medal positions, we're awaiting the results."

"Just don't let it be the Germans," Jimmy said. "Maybe the Yanks won, Da."

"I don't know, Jimbo. They had a lot of ground to make up."

The announcer filled the time waiting for the final results by recapping the race. Even Kimberly put her knitting on the coffee table and leaned forward, feet on the floor.

"What's taking so long?" Kimberly asked.

Jimmy and I looked at her and laughed.

"Can't a woman be interested in the outcome?" she asked.

"Of course," Jimmy said. "I just didn't know you were listening."

Kimberly furrowed her brow and let out a little grunt, which made Jimmy laugh even more.

The announcer's voice became louder and more excited. "…judge is stepping to the microphone." There was a pause, and then a German-accented voice shouted, "United States."

Jimmy jumped to his feet. "If it couldn't be the Brits, I'm happy the Yanks won." He pumped his fist in the air.

Kimberly sighed and sat back. "You must be happy," she said to me, smiling.

"Why would I be happy?" I asked.

"It's your home," she said. "You should be happy."

"You're my home," I said.

Kimberly blew me a kiss. I did the same.

"Wowza," Jimmy said. "Would you like me to leave the two of you alone?"

Chapter 27
(1937)

We were in the living room listening to George Gershwin's "Rhapsody in Blue" on the radio. I read the newspaper and Kimberly flipped through a magazine. Every few minutes, she got up and looked out the front window.

"I think it's raining harder now," she said. "Why do they practice when it's raining so hard?"

Jimmy was at football practice and should have been home by now. If I had to guess, he didn't want to ride his bike home in the heavy rain, so he holed up at the club until the rain let up a bit.

"The boy will be fine. He'll be home soon."

Kimberly sat back and picked up her magazine.

"He shouldn't be riding his bike in this rain. He could get hit by a car or lose control."

I folded the newspaper and set it on the coffee table. "Love, would you like a cup of tea?"

Kimberly jumped to her feet. "I'll make it." She rushed off.

A minute or two after leaving the room, Kimberly came back in and looked out the front window.

"I thought you were going to make tea," I said.

"I put the kettle on. I just wanted to see how hard it's raining now."

I grunted a response, stood, and went to the window, walking up behind Kimberly. I put my arms around her and nuzzled her neck. "Relax. When the rain stops, Jimmy will be home and all will be right with the world."

Kimberly let out a nervous giggle. "Of course, he will," she said. "I just wish he'd hurry."

The kettle whistled, and Kimberly broke herself from my embrace. "I'd better get that."

I followed her into the kitchen and got cups and saucers ready while she tended to the kettle.

"You know, I don't like being this way," she said, her back to me. "I just have this fear, this feeling of dread, that I can't seem to shake."

I went to her and turned her toward me. "I know. I wish there was something I could say or do to make it all better for you. All I can tell you is that everything is going to be alright. Jimmy is going to be alright."

Kimberly hugged me, then turned her attention to the tea. She poured us each a cup and we took our tea into the living room. I sat in my chair. Kimberly set her cup on the coffee table then checked the front window again. The rain had let up. She was about to sit when the kitchen door opened, and Jimmy came inside. Kimberly rushed to him.

The moment she saw him, she said, "You're going to catch your death of cold. Stay there. I'll get you a towel." Kimberly ran upstairs to get a towel and I wandered into the kitchen.

"How was practice?" I asked.

"Wet." Jimmy sat at the kitchen table taking off his shoes and socks. "Then on the way home, I nearly got hit by a car."

I shook my head. "Maybe it's best you not tell Mum about that."

Chapter 28
(1939)

Jeffrey lit a cigarette, took a deep drag, then pointed at me. "I think you're wrong, mate. Hitler's crazy, but he's not stupid. He won't invade Poland." He drew a beer from the tap and set it in front of me. It was mid-afternoon, and except for a few employees, The Blue Note was empty.

I took a drink. "That's what people said when he threatened to take back the Rhineland, and then Austria. When he marched into Czechoslovakia, everyone said Hitler was satisfied. But I'm telling you, he's not satisfied. He wants all of Europe."

We had watched as Germany took over the Rhineland in 1936, invaded Austria in 1938, and just a month earlier had taken over Czechoslovakia. England, the United States, and the rest of the world sat back and allowed it to happen. I was convinced that if no one stood up to Hitler, Poland was next, and I doubted if that would be the end of his desires.

"Chamberlain has threatened to go to war if Hitler invades Poland. He doesn't want the Brits and the French coming after him. I tell you, he won't step foot in Poland." Jeffrey moved the cigarette to the corner of his mouth and drew a beer for himself.

I took a big slug of my beer, then shook my head. "He wants it all. Just wait until he comes after England."

"Now you're talking nonsense, mate" Jeffrey said.

"He's a maniac," I said.

"I hope you're wrong, Boss. Maybe I should just go over there and kick some Jerry ass myself." Jeffrey raised his hands like a boxer.

"That sounds like a workable plan." I raised my beer in a toast. "I'll ring up the prime minister to let him know you're on your way." I put my mug up to my ear like I was talking on a phone. "Neville, it's Henry. No need to worry about Hitler. Jeffrey is on his way to Germany to gives those Huns what for."

Jeffrey laughed, his cigarette bobbing up and down in his mouth. "I just might do that," he said.

I finished my beer and slid the mug toward Jeffrey.

"Another?" he asked.

"No, I need to get home. Jimmy is graduating from secondary school tonight, and we're taking him out to celebrate."

"Tell the little bugger I said congratulations. Is he still planning on going to Oxford?"

"He has offers from Oxford and University College. He's still trying to make up his mind."

"He's a smart one, just like his mother." Jeffrey winked and smiled.

"Too true." I waved and walked out.

Chapter 29
(1939)

At dinner, I ordered a Tanqueray and tonic for myself and a gimlet for Kimberly. "You're a graduate now, Jimbo. Would you like a drink?"

Jimmy smiled. "How about a Guinness?"

"The lad fancies a Guinness." I gave the waiter a wink.

"Very good, sir," the waiter said, then scurried away.

"Just one, Jimmy," Kimberly said. "You may fancy a Guinness, but I don't fancy you drinking."

"He's growing up, Mum," I said. "He needs to learn how to drink before he goes off to university."

Jimmy's smile faded. "I wanted to talk to you both about that."

The waiter brought our drinks. Jimmy grew nervous, took a drink of the Guinness, then wiped his mouth with the back of his hand.

"I know you were hoping I'd go to university," he said. But I'm thinking about joining the RAF."

"The Air Force?" Kimberly asked, grabbing my arm.

I put my hand over Kimberly's. "Why would you do that, Jim?"

"There are rumors that the government is going to bring back the full draft, not the limited one we have now. They're going to need soldiers if Hitler invades Poland, and we go to war. I'd like to join the RAF and become a pilot before there's a mad rush of draftees."

"I've heard the rumors," I said. "I've also heard that university students will be exempted from the draft."

"I don't want to avoid the draft, Da."

Kimberly raised her glass and her hand shook. It took a moment for her to calm herself before she could drink.

"Are you all right, Mum?" Jimmy asked.

Kimberly forced a smile. She was on the verge of tears.

"I'm sorry if I upset you, Mum, but I feel like I can do more good for England in the RAF than I can at university."

"Let's talk about this later," I said. "Tonight should be a celebration. We'll worry about tomorrow tomorrow."

The waiter returned. We ordered more drinks and dinner, but the joy had been sucked out of the evening.

Chapter 30
(1939)

When we got home from the restaurant, Kimberly went to our bedroom and cried. The sound of her sobbing echoed through the house.

Jimmy was out with friends, so Kimberly and I were alone. I sat in the living room listening to the radio, waiting for her to come downstairs. When she didn't, I went upstairs to talk to her.

She was on the bed, staring at the ceiling. The sobbing was done, but tears rolled down her cheeks. "We have to stop him," she said.

"I'm not sure we can." I spoke softly, my voice as calm as I could make it.

"He's just a child."

"We don't know that there's going to be a war."

"You've been saying for months that Hitler's not going to stop until someone stops him."

I silently cursed myself. "Maybe I'm wrong." I paused, hesitant to say what I truly thought. "And Love, Jimmy isn't a child anymore."

Kimberly sat up with a fierce look in her eyes. "You want him to go to war?"

I held up my hands in defense. "Of course not. I just…" I dropped my hands and exhaled deeply. "I don't think there's anything we can do to stop him."

Kimberly's demeanor softened. "We have to try. You'll talk to him, won't you?"

"I will." I wanted to say more, to make Kimberly understand, to not get her hopes up. But I couldn't find the words. "I will."

***

We had lunch at the Hare and Hound. The waiter asked if we wanted drinks, and without hesitating, Jimmy ordered a Guiness.

"You like your Guiness, do you, son?"

Jimmy nodded and smiled.

"Alright then, I'll have a Guiness, too."

The waiter left. Jimmy and I had had a million conversations about things great and small, but I felt completely unprepared for this conversation.

"I wanted to talk to you about your plans to join the RAF," I said.

"Go on," Jimmy said.

"It's a big decision, Jimbo. I don't know if we're going to go to war with Germany, but if we do, the RAF is going to be in the thick of it."

Jimmy nodded, listening patiently.

"You're a smart lad, and you have options."

The waiter brought our beers. I took a long pull from mine.

"If you go to university and they allow deferments for university students, you could avoid this whole mess. Plus, you'd come out the other side with a degree." Before the words were out of my mouth, I knew what Jimmy's response was going to be.

"It's my duty to serve." Jimmy spoke calmly. "I've also heard that if we do go to war with Germany, Parliament isn't going to allow student deferments. I want to get in and be trained as a pilot before the masses are drafted in."

I nodded. I almost couldn't blame him for wanting to join. Even so, I felt desperate to convince him to choose another option.

"Jim, we could move to the United States. You could go to university there. We could stay there until the war is over…if there is war."

Jimmy laughed. "You're pulling out all of the stops, aren't you?" He took a drink and became more serious. "Da, I don't want to run away. I'm a proud son of England. When she calls, I want to answer."

"But she's not calling yet."

Jimmy smiled and lowered his voice. "I can hear her whisper, Da."

Although I envied his sense of obligation to defend his homeland, I didn't like what I was hearing.

"You've already made up your mind, haven't you?" I asked.

Jimmy smiled. "I signed up to join day before yesterday."

Chapter 31
(1939)

As I feared, Germany invaded Poland in September 1938. Chamberlain gave Hitler every opportunity to step back from the brink, but Chamberlain was weak, his threats impotent. Two days after Hitler invaded Poland, Great Britain declared war on Germany. Had Jimmy not joined the RAF when he did, he would have been drafted.

Kimberly went to the post box every day looking for a letter from Jimmy. When none came, she spent the day sulking. If we did get a letter, she would tear it open and read it aloud to me. Once she finished, she would read it again to herself.

One morning, after working in the garden, I came in to find Kimberly waiting with an unopened letter from Jimmy.

"Let me wash up," I said. "Then you can read it to me."

"No, sit down." She pointed at the kitchen table.

I knew better than to argue.

Kimberly read excitedly. As usual, Jimmy was good, his mates were brilliant, the food wasn't very good, but they got a lot of it. The big news was that Jimmy now flew a Submarine Spitfire, a single-seater fighter plane, rather than the de Haviland Tiger Moth he was first trained in. He said it was the best plane in the RAF arsenal.

Jimmy may have been excited, but Kimberly was not. To her, this meant his time safe in training was now over. When she finished reading, she handed it to me and walked out of the kitchen.

I still had dirt all over my hands and shoes. After I cleaned up, I found Kimberly sitting on Jimmy's bed. She did not look up when I walked in.

She held Jimmy's pillow, rocking back and forth. I thought about reaching out to comfort her but knew nothing I did or said could ease her mind. I let her be and went downstairs to listen to music.

Chapter 32
(1940)

Every night for a month, German bombs rained down on London. The Blue Note operated even as the bombs began to fall, but within a week, with bombs hitting close by and England instituting a 'no lights' policy, we shut down.

Kimberly often sat silently in Jimmy's bedroom with the curtains pulled and the lights off. I tried to coax her downstairs to eat something, but after a while, I stopped trying.

When the bombing migrated west toward Osterley, I told her we should head into London to seek shelter, but she wanted to stay home, close to Jimmy's things.

"If the Germans start dropping bombs here," I said, "there'll be nowhere for us to hide."

"No." She turned her back to me.

The following day, I went out to the post box and was surprised to find a letter from Jimmy. Since the bombing started, we hadn't heard from him.

"Come downstairs, Love. We got a letter from Jimmy. I'll read it to you."

Her dark eyes lit up. "A letter?" She happily followed me downstairs.

We wanted to know where Jimmy was. Was he staying safe? But his letter didn't go into the details we wanted. He said he was doing well and claimed he and his mates "had the Jerrys on the run," although it didn't feel like that to those of us on the ground.

Despite the lack of specifics, Kimberly's spirits were lifted, and her mood brightened. She sat on the couch reading over the letter again and again. I watched her and was struck by how rail thin she had become, and how unkempt her hair was. It appeared to have not been washed in days.

When she finished reading the letter, she carefully folded it and put it back in the envelope. "I'm going to put this upstairs." She stored all Jimmy's letters in a small box she kept in his room. "When I'm done, I'll come down and make tea."

She seldom stepped foot in the kitchen since Jimmy got his wings. I made our meals—which Kimberly seldom ate—and I took to having tea alone. I smiled at Kimberly, pleased to see her take some initiative. "That would be wonderful."

***

As the days passed and the bombs continued to fall, Kimberly slipped back into the dark place she had retreated to previously. I was back to spending my time alone.

Christmas was just a few days away, but we had not decorated the way we had when Jimmy was home. Without him with us, it didn't feel at all like the holidays. I suspected Kimberly's dark mood had something to do with Jimmy not being home at Christmastime.

I was cleaning up the kitchen when there was a knock on the front door. I assumed Kimberly would get it, but the knocking continued. When I walked into the living room, I found her standing at the bottom of the stairs.

"Are you going to get the door?" I asked.

She shook her head, her gaze fixed on the front door.

"For goodness sakes," I opened the door and found a man holding a telegram. My heart sank.

"Mister Ross?" the man asked. "I have a telegram for you." The man handed me the envelope and quickly walked away.

I held the telegram with both hands, as if it might shatter if I dropped it. I turned toward Kimberly.

"It's a telegram." My voice was soft and seemed distant.

Kimberly stood motionless. Tears welled up in her eyes.

I pulled the telegram out of the envelope and read out loud.

FROM AIR MINISTRY P695 DEEPLY REGRET TO INFORM YOU THAT YOUR SON FLYING OFFICER JAMES PATRICK ROSS IS REPORTED AS HAVING LOST HIS LIFE AS THE RESULT OF AIR OPERATIONS STOP LETTER FOLLOWS STOP THE AIR COUNCIL EXPRESS THEIR PROFOUND SYMPATHY

My voice quavered and trailed off with the last few words.

Kimberly collapsed. I cradled her and carried her to the couch, surprised she had become nothing more than skin and bones. She had not fainted. Her eyes were open, but she was unresponsive. She neither sobbed nor wailed. Tears streamed down her stoic face, and as I held her in my arms, I felt the sensation that she was a million miles away.

Chapter 33
(1940)

I awoke to Kimberly's wail. This had been going on for a few days. Except to go to the loo, Kimberly had not left the couch, spending her days staring blankly at the ceiling.

I took to sleeping in the chair, worried about my wife and wanting to be near her.

Then, late one afternoon as the sun set, an explosion rocked the house. I was upstairs changing clothes. I ran to the bedroom window. Smoke and flames rose near Eversley Crescent, several hundred meters from our house. The bombing had come to Osterley.

"Kimberly, we have to go."

She just stared at the ceiling.

I grabbed her arm and tried to help her stand, but she resisted. "Kimberly, please."

She pulled her arm away and looked straight ahead. Her eyes were dark and disconnected.

"We have to go." I picked her up and carried her to our car. Air raid sirens sounded, piercing the late December afternoon. I looked around to see if any of our neighbors were getting in their cars and heading toward London, but I knew that most of them had left days earlier. We should have done the same.

The closer we got to the city, the worse the roadway got, pockmarked with potholes and debris from earlier bombings. Half-destroyed buildings lined the roadway, their remains toppled out into the road.

The street leading to Clapham South Underground Station on Nightengale Lane—the one closest to our home—was blocked by debris. Air raid sirens filled the otherwise quiet night.

I made a U-turn and tried going around the block to Malwood Road. Darkness had taken over, and I could not bring myself to turn on the headlights. Headlights—any lights—were forbidden, and I did not want to make our vehicle a target. I steered around the burned-out carcass of a car on my left and drove into a deep hole in the road. I felt something in the steering break. I tried to back up, but the car wouldn't budge.

"We're almost there. We can walk from here. Let's go."

Kimberly remained in her seat, silent. Despite the scream of the air raid sirens, the skies above appeared clear and free of enemy bombers. Even so, a bomb exploded nearby, the impact knocking me to the ground.

I struggled to my feet and sprinted around to the passenger side of the car to help Kimberly, who still refused to move. "Please, Kimberly. We have to go."

Another explosion stole my breath and turned the world temporarily dark. When I woke, I was on the ground. Through smoke in the air and tears in my eyes, I saw the shape of my car across the street. The car was covered with bricks and debris.

"Kimberly," I called out, but my wife's name came out in a whisper. I tried again and again. I attempted to stand, but my legs didn't want to work. I dragged myself toward the car, reaching out with my hands, pulling my body forward, but making precious little progress. I felt the energy drain from my body and my vision blackened. The darkness closed in until it finally consumed me.

Chapter 34
(1940)

I opened my eyes and saw a shape, a person, standing over me. "Kimberly?" My mouth was dry. The word came out garbled, indistinct.

"Relax, Love." It was a woman's voice, but not Kimberly's. "You're in hospital. You've been injured."

"Where's Kimberly?" The words didn't sound right.

"I'll get the doctor," the voice said, then walked away.

I tried to sit up, but my body wasn't cooperating. A hand patted my shoulder, and I looked up to see a different shape. My vision was improving. This shape appeared to be a man with gray hair.

"Just lie back." He took my hand and checked my pulse, then held a pen up in front of my face. "Can you follow this as I move it?"

I moved my head to follow the pen.

"No, no. Don't move your head. Just your eye."

I did as I was told, blinking to try to improve my vision. "Where's my wife? She was in the car."

"That will be all, nurse," the doctor said, then pulled a chair up next to the bed. He wore glasses, and had thick, bushy eyebrows. He looked at a clipboard, and then at me. "Mr. Ross, my name is Doctor Chambers. You were found out in the street a little over a week ago. You were badly injured, and you were lying next to a car. There was a woman in the car. I assume that was your wife."

"Kimberly."

"I'm sorry, Mr. Ross, but the woman was not alive when you were found."

I reached up to wipe away the tears and felt a bandage over my left eye. "What is this?" I asked.

"As I said, you were seriously injured. You have a broken leg, and two broken ribs. You also suffered a nasty blow to the head, and I'm afraid you've lost an eye. We tried to save it, but the damage was too severe."

I tried again to sit up. I wanted to get out of bed and as far away from the hospital as possible. A pain shot through my entire body, and I collapsed back onto the bed. I let out a moan.

The doctor put his hand on my shoulder and held me down, "It's too soon for that," he said. "You'll need to…"

The doctor's voice seemed to be getting farther away. But I had already heard all I needed to hear. Kimberly was dead. Jimmy was dead. I closed my eyes and welcomed the darkness.

Chapter 35
(1941)

I walked out of the hospital and was surprised that the weather was warm. My last memory of being outside was the night Kimberly was killed. It was winter, and the sky had been gray, the air cold. Now, it was summer, and although the sky was overcast, the air was warm and welcoming.

The streets around the hospital were still clogged with debris, but the constant German bombing had stopped while I was still confined to a hospital bed.

My leg had healed, but I still didn't have my strength back. I limped slowly, making my way as best I could.

My plan was to go home, but my car was destroyed, and my weak legs could not make it that far. The only possibility was to walk several blocks to The Blue Note with the hope that someone would be there with a car.

I walked for two blocks before I had to stop to rest. In several places, the sidewalks were blocked with debris. Bricks and cement blocks were mixed with charred timbers, bits of twisted metal, and the material refuse of thousands of ruined lives. As I continued my journey, I tried not to think about what had happened to the people that once lived and worked in the crumbled buildings.

Finally at The Blue Note, I saw nothing more than a pile of rubble. The tall building next door had fallen and crushed it. The back wall was still standing, but the other walls had collapsed. The bar was buried beneath a pile of bricks from the neighboring building. Tables and chairs were broken and strewn around the rubble. My beloved grand piano lay broken and useless.

I looked away. It was just one more tragedy in a long line of tragedies that had taken over my once wonderful life.

I walked away, wandering aimlessly for a few blocks until I came to what appeared to be a convoy of military vehicles on the side of the road. I stood next to one of the big trucks and stared.

"What you looking at there, mate?"

I turned to see a soldier smoking a cigarette.

"What?"

"I asked what you're looking at? You was staring up at the transport like you seen a ghost." The soldier had three stripes on the shoulder of his uniform indicating he was a sergeant.

"I was just looking." My voice sounded soft and distant.

"You're a Yank," the sergeant said. "What are you doing here?"

"I live here, well, out in Osterley. I need a ride to my house."

The sergeant took a final puff of his cigarette, tossed it in front of him, and ground it with his boot. "We got some trucks going out to the Aerodrome. They could maybe drop you off on the way. That is, if you don't mind riding in the back of one of these devils."

"I don't mind," I said.

The sergeant walked over to another man in uniform. The other man nodded, and the sergeant returned to me. "The lieutenant said you can ride along, mate, but they're leaving right now. Are you ready to go?"

I told him I was ready, and he helped me climb into the back of a transport truck where eight or ten soldiers were waiting.

"Take care of this bloke," the sergeant said. "He's a Yank."

"Yes, sergeant," the soldiers in the truck said, and then became quiet.

I sat on a metal bench that ran along each side of the back of the truck. The truck bed was covered with a green canvas roof that protected the soldiers from the weather. It smelled of sweat, diesel fuel, and smoke.

"The sarge says you're a Yank," the soldier sitting next to me said. "Why're you in London?"

I thought about what had brought me to London, what had happened to Kimberly. I didn't want to think about it. "I was in hospital," I said. "I hurt my leg." I didn't even think about the black patch over my left eye.

The soldier nodded, then fell silent.

The truck pulled down the road, occasionally swerving to miss debris or dropping a wheel into a pothole. It took more effort than it should have to stay on the metal bench and not bounce around too much. The roads were less rough and rutted the farther we drove. I closed my eye and tried to shut out the smell and movement of the truck, both of which made me nauseous. I felt like I might fall asleep, but every time the truck hit a bump or one of the soldiers spoke, I opened my eye. Finally, the truck came to a stop and the sergeant came around to the back.

"This is your stop," the sergeant said.

We had stopped on the M4 near the Osterley House Mansion, where the Home Guard had once trained. I was still a mile or so from home but was thankful to be that close.

The sergeant reached up and helped me out of the back of the truck. The climb down was more difficult than I anticipated.

"Thank you, Sergeant."

"Anything for a Yank." The sergeant walked back to the cab of the truck, and the convoy pulled away.

I walked toward home with my head down, breathing heavily from the effort. I thought about being back home, sleeping in my own bed. I tried to think about positive things, to keep my energy up, but my thoughts kept turning to Kimberly and Jimmy. I wanted to get home, but I knew they wouldn't be there. They would never again be there.

By the time I made it to my street, I was exhausted. The neighborhood looked different. Bombs had damaged some of the houses and knocked down several trees. When I came around the curve and saw my house, I stopped and stared. There was a crater in the ground where the front porch had been. The front of the house had collapsed, and there was evidence of a fire. I stood and stared at the home I had shared with Kimberly and Jimmy. The war had taken that too.

I walked around back and found the door ajar. I pushed it open and was greeted with the smell of burned wood and plastic. The smell was nauseating. The light from outside lit up the interior of the home, and I could see that the fire had damaged much of the first floor. The charred remains of my life—our lives—littered the interior of the home.

The second floor was not damaged as badly as the first, although the sickening smell was still strong. I stood at the top of the stairs, unable to make my way further into what had once been my home.

I retreated to the garden, where the grass had grown long and wispy in my absence. The garden shed, which had survived the bombing without damage, stood forlornly, welcoming me. I removed the Qualcast roller mower from the shed, as well as the rakes, spades and other garden tools, and placed everything along the side of the shed, opening up some space inside.

Eventually., I felt the urge to try once again and returned to the house. This time, I walked slowly toward Jimmy's room. The impact from the bombs had knocked things off Jimmy's shelves. On the floor near the bed, I found the box of letters from Jimmy that Kimberly had kept. I knelt, and picked up each letter, placing them back in the box. It took considerable effort to stand, but when I did, I placed the box of letters back on the shelf. I patted the box and stood silently, catching my breath.

I yanked the mattress off Jimmy's bed and lugged it down to the garden shed. That would be my new home, at least temporarily. The effort exhausted me.

I returned to the house and found two blankets in a closet that had not been damaged by the fire. They smelled slightly of smoke, but they would have to do. I took them out to the shed and spread one over the mattress. It was late afternoon, but I craved sleep. I curled up on the mattress and covered myself with the remaining blanket. I closed my eyes and sleep came quickly.

Chapter 36
(1941)

I woke to the sound of rain on the roof of the shed and to water dripping on my forehead. I sat up in a panic, taking a moment to figure out where I was. The shed was completely dark. There wasn't much room inside, but I managed to move the mattress closer to the door. In no time, I was back asleep.

I next woke shivering. I wriggled under the blanket I had been lying on top of, but even with two blankets, it remained uncomfortably chilly. The rain had stopped, and I could see the first rays of morning sunlight coming through cracks between the sideboards of the shed. I craved more sleep, but when it became clear that the cold wasn't going to allow it, I climbed out from under the blankets and went outside to find some wood to start a fire.

I gathered a few small sticks at the back of the garden but needed something more substantial. I walked to the front of the house and pried broken boards away from the collapsed porch. I collected several broken two-by-fours and a few pieces of broken plywood, then carried them back to the shed.

I used the spade I had removed from the shed the day before and dug a hole in the garden. The dirt was soft from the overnight rain and digging was easy. Once I had a hole six or eight inches deep and a couple of feet across, I piled the small sticks into the hole and crossed three of the two-by-fours teepee-style across the kindling. I fished a book of matches out of my pocket. It had The Blue Note logo on the front. I struck the match on the strike strip, but the match would not ignite. I tried again but had the same result. I threw the match into the hole with the wood and tried another one. I only had three matches left. I struck the next match, and it lit on the first try. I held the flame against the thin kindling, but it wouldn't light. I tried an even thinner part of the sticks, but still could not get the fire to catch. The match was burning down, and as I held it to the wood, it burned my fingertips.

"Bloody hell!" I stuck my injured finger in my mouth to cool.

I went into the shed and found a stack of old Modern Wonder magazines. Jimmy had been a fan of the magazine, which had a color cover and newspaper print pages. I ripped out several pages from one of the magazines and crumpled them up into a loose ball, then placed the paper in the hole with the kindling. I lit another match. When I put the match to paper, the newsprint immediately set alight and began to burn. I blew on the flame, and it rose, lighting the kindling. The orange flame grew, and a few minutes later, the two-by-fours began to burn as well.

I retrieved a wooden chair from the patio and dragged it next to the fire. I was going to sit to warm my cold, tired body, but thought better of it. I needed to eat and knew that I should keep moving rather than sit in the chair. I went into the house to see if I could find any food.

Fire had destroyed much of the kitchen, leaving everything in the pantry charred and useless. I searched through the cupboards, but there was no food that could be salvaged.

I went outside to the cellar door. The twin wooden doors were held shut with a metal rod that ran between the handle of each door. I removed the rod and opened the doors. A wet, musty smell like decaying plants escaped the cellar. It had been months since anyone had gone down there, so the smell was even stronger than usual. We had kept a garden where we grew beans and carrots and other vegetables. Kimberly canned what we didn't eat, but I could not recall her canning any vegetables from the previous year's crop. Once Jimmy joined the RAF, she had been too despondent to do much of anything.

The cellar was dark. I lit a match, and the cellar lit up in a soft glow. On the shelves were four or five glass jars. I grabbed them as quickly as I could before the match burned down. As I gathered the jars, I dropped the match and it extinguished when it hit the dirt floor. I was in total darkness. I hugged the jars against my body with my left hand and felt along the shelves and walls with my right. I moved slowly toward the stairs, and after taking a few steps, saw the light from outside coming through the open cellar door. I moved with more confidence toward the light, then exited the cellar with four jars of vegetables.

I sat in the patio chair next to the fire and surveyed my newfound treasure. I had two jars of pickled carrots, a jar of green beans, and a jar of beets. I hated pickled carrots and set those aside. I twisted the lid to the green beans and noticed that the mason jar had cracked near the top. There was no liquid inside. I removed the lid and smelled the beans. They smelled sour and spoiled. I plucked a bean out of the jar and tasted it. It was putrid, and I spit it out into the fire.

"Damn it." I spit again, trying to get the taste out of my mouth.

That left the beets. I took the lid off the jar and pulled out a slice of beet. The jar was full of liquid and the beet smelled earthy, like dirt after a rain. The smell reminded me of childhood. I thought about being out in the country when I was young, when Philip and Mother were still alive, the smell of the plowed fields a mixture of rich earth and fresh spring air.

I wondered what my life would have been like if I hadn't come to Europe after graduation. I'd probably be in Chicago, with a job and a wife, a child or two. The war would be so far away.

I shook my head. This was my reality now. Kimberly was gone, Jimmy was gone, and all I could do was try to survive, even if that meant sleeping in a shed and eating canned beets. I let out a sarcastic laugh and shook my head again. I put the beet in my mouth and was pleasantly surprised. It tasted good.

The cloud cover was beginning to burn off and the day was brightening. I sat back in the wooden chair and ate more of the beets, then screwed the lid back on the mason jar. Even though I was extremely hungry, I didn't want to eat all the beets at once because I was unsure where my next meal would come from. I limped into the shed and put the jar on a shelf. I retrieved the jars of carrots and took them into the shed, placing them alongside the beets. I hoped things didn't become so desperate that I had to eat the pickled carrots.

I sat back in the chair and let out a long sigh. Gathering wood, starting a fire, and hunting for food had tired me out. My leg ached and I considered going back to bed for more sleep. Instead, I stretched out in the chair and allowed the sun to warm my face. The day was heating up, and it felt good sitting in the sun.

What was next? I thought about rebuilding the house, but quickly gave up on that idea. Because of rationing, the materials needed to do the repairs wouldn't be available. And besides, did I really want to stay here without Kimberly and Jimmy? Maybe it was best not to think about such things. I felt like I was getting ahead of myself. Those decisions could wait. The first thing I needed to do was heal my body, then I could worry about the future.

When the sun went down, I moved back into the shed and lit a small candle I had scavenged from the house. It provided enough light so it wasn't completely dark in the shed, but not enough to allow me to read one of the Modern Wonder magazines. I tried to keep my mind off Kimberly and Jimmy and what my future might look like, but no matter what I thought about, my mind kept coming back to one of those three things.

I wondered what Jimmy thought just before he died. Did he know he was going to die or was he unaware? Was his death painful?

"Enough," I said out loud. My voice was loud and harsh in the darkened shed.

I leaned forward in my chair and rested my head in my hands. There would be time in the future to consider all the questions that were coursing through my mind. For now, I needed to focus on surviving.

I wiped my forehead and was surprised to find that I was sweating heavily. After sundown, the air had cooled. Even so, I was surprisingly hot.

"I hope those beets weren't bad," I said out loud.

I got out of the chair and lay on the mattress. Even though it wasn't very late, I was tired and decided to sleep. Morning would come soon enough, and I would have to find something else to eat.

I rolled over and was surprised to see light pouring in through the shed doors. I was disoriented. Why were the doors open? Why was the sun up? I stood and immediately felt dizzy. I leaned heavily against the wall and grabbed the shelving to keep from falling. When I regained my balance, I walked out of the shed and was greeted by a bright, hot sun. Had I slept through the night?

I looked around, but the sun made it difficult to see anything. Everything was too bright, too out of focus. I could make out things close by—the shed, the fire pit, the tree that stood next to the shed—but I could not make out objects in the distance. Even the house was just a dark indistinct blob.

I was so hot I felt like I was burning up. I thought about the beets. Were they off? Could eating a few bad beets make me feel this bad? I needed help, so I crossed the yard and stumbled through the neighbor's hedges. The Cromwells could help if I could get to their house. Nancy, the woman who had watched Jimmy a few times, was a nurse. She would know what to do. But the yard was so big, and from the look of it, the grass had not been mowed in quite some time.

I walked carefully through the grass, feeling unsteady and overheated. I watched my feet cut through the grass, making sure I did not trip. But when I looked up, the Cromwell's house was still so far away. I focused on the house, willing myself to get to it. Finally, I made it to the Cromwell's back door and rang the bell. When no one answered, I knocked politely. Still, no one answered the door, so I knocked loudly with the side of my fist. I banged harder and harder until my hand hurt.

"Hello? Anyone? I need help."

No one answered.

I sat down on the back stoop. I either could go back to the shed and wait for whatever I was experiencing to pass, or I could go to hospital in London. The hospital was so far away, but I needed help. What if my illness didn't pass?

I badly wanted to lie down, but the thought scared me. What if I went back to the shed to sleep, but then could not get back up? I struggled to my feet, glanced across the yard at the shed and the house I once shared with my family, and walked around to the front of the Cromwell's house. I stood for a moment to catch my breath, then walked down their driveway and out to the road.

My limp was more pronounced and my leg more painful. I began walking toward Osterley House, where the military transport had dropped me off two days earlier. My hope was that I could catch a ride into London on the M4. Maybe the sergeant would come by in his big truck and pick me up.

When I reached Osterley House, I collapsed in the grass of their expansive garden. My leg alternatively ached, then felt numb. I rolled onto my back and stared up into the sky. Clouds blocked the sun, but it was still so hot. Even so, I was shivering, as if it was cold. That was odd, I thought, but then the thought was gone.

I rolled over and saw people in the distance. They were indistinct, just shapes, I forced myself up onto my feet and stumbled toward them. I was dragging my leg now, and each step took tremendous effort.

When I got to where the people had been, I realized I hadn't seen any people after all. What I saw were cars driving past on the M4. I stood on the side of the roadway and put my thumb out like I had done when hitchhiking in college. A car came by and swerved, honking its horn. What was I doing out in the roadway? I moved to the shoulder, dragging my leg, and put my thumb out again. I stood that way for some time before I realized that no cars were coming.

I waited, and two more cars came by close together. I stuck out my thumb, but the cars whizzed by.

When the next car approached, I stood up straight and tried to smile. I put my hand up and stuck out my thumb. The car slowed, and then rolled past me, coming to a stop twenty meters up the road. I walked toward the car as fast as I could, but my leg didn't want to cooperate. I dragged the leg, and finally made it to the passenger side of the car. The door opened, but there was a man already in the seat.

"Need a ride?" he asked in a Scottish brogue.

"Yes," I said, confused. "I need to get to London."

"Right, that's where I'm going. Why don't you get in the other side?"

I nodded, and using the car for balance, walked to the door on the other side.

The Scotsman told me his name, but I immediately forgot it. He offered his hand.

"I'm Henry Ross." I shook the man's hand and felt weak.

The man put the car in gear and pulled back out onto the road. Pain radiated from my bad leg. I rubbed it and felt a needle-like tingle wherever I rubbed.

The man was talking to me, but I couldn't focus on what he was saying.

"…this bloody war is ever going to end…Churchill will send us all… Germans can't hold out…look pale, lad. Are you feeling all right?"

The man's voice was an echo coming from a million miles away. I closed my eye and thought about Kimberly. I needed to get home to her. She would be waiting.

Chapter 37
(1941)

I opened my eye and saw I was back in hospital. A man stood next to my bed. A familiar face.

"Doctor Chambers?"

He looked up from his clipboard and adjusted his glasses. "Mr. Ross, you enjoyed our hospitality so much that you've returned. How nice."

"I'm back in hospital."

"Indeed, you are."

"Why? What happened?" I asked.

The doctor wrote something on his clipboard, then turned his attention to me. "A nice chap dropped you off. Said you passed out in his car."

I barely remembered the Scotsman who had picked me up on the M4. "I mean, what's wrong with me? Why am I here?"

"I'm afraid that you picked up an infection in your leg. We're treating that with antibiotics, and you should be fine in a day or two. The other problem is that you were dehydrated. That's easy to treat, but were you eating and drinking enough when you left us earlier this week?"

"I had some beets."

"Man was not meant to live by beets alone, Mr. Ross." The doctor smiled.

I told him about my damaged home, how I didn't have access to more food.

The doctor returned the clipboard to a hook on the foot of the bed. "I see. Try to get some rest now. I'll be back a little later to check on you."

I did as I was instructed, quickly drifting off to sleep. When I awoke, the room was dark, and a nurse was taking my pulse. I wanted more sleep and closed my eye again. When I next woke, bright sunlight filled the room. I felt much better. My leg had stopped throbbing, and I felt stronger and more clear-headed.

A woman pushing a cart and wearing a pink and white striped uniform walked by the foot of my bed. "Would you like some breakfast, Love?"

"Yes, thank you."

The woman took a tray from her cart and placed it in front of me. It contained a plate with two fried eggs, link sausage, toast, baked beans, and fried tomatoes. I eagerly dug into my breakfast.

As I was finishing my meal, Doctor Chambers came in. He stopped to talk to a couple other patients, then came to me.

"Looks like you were a bit hungry." Chambers pointed at my empty plate. "I hope it was good."

"Not too good, but there was plenty of it," I said.

The doctor laughed. "How are we feeling this morning?"

"Much better than yesterday."

"That's good," the doctor said. "Do you feel up to leaving us this morning?"

"No offense, but I'm anxious to get out of here."

"I can understand that." The doctor took a business card out of his shirt pocket and handed it to me. "This is for a friend of mine. He owns a boarding house just a few blocks from here. It's not very fancy, but it's better than a garden shed." He winked.

"Thank you," I said. "I hadn't even thought about where I'd go when I left."

The doctor nodded. "Good luck, Mr. Ross." He gave a slight wave, then moved down the row of beds to another patient.

Chapter 38
(1941)

The house was two stories tall and painted gray. There was a handwritten note taped over the doorbell that read "Don't Work." I knocked on the dark wooden front door. My effort barely made a sound, so I knocked harder. An old man with stooped shoulders and thin, gray hair opened the door.

"Can I help you?" the man asked in a weak, reedy voice.

"I'm looking for a room," I said. "My home was destroyed, and I need a place to stay."

"Did Ian Chambers send you?"

It took me a second to place the name. "Yes. Doctor Chambers. He sent me."

"Ian rang me up about you. Come in." The old man held the door open, and we walked into a dark foyer. It took a moment for my good eye to adjust to the darkness. To the left was a stairway, and straight ahead was a white-painted wooden door.

"I have one room available," he said. "It's upstairs. Would you like to see it?"

"I would."

The old man motioned for me to follow, then slowly led the way upstairs, taking each step deliberately. At the top of the stairs, the man paused to catch his breath, then continued down the hallway past two closed doors. At a third door, the man stopped, fished a key out of his pocket, and opened the door.

The room was small and dark, with a thin, stained mattress on a spring frame, a scarred dresser, a small nightstand, and a narrow closet in the corner. The old man turned on a single overhead light that hung down from the ceiling, then walked across the room. He raised a window shade, revealing a dirty, yellowed window that looked out onto the side garden and the neighbor's home beyond. The room smelled old and musty, reminding me of my first apartment in Paris.

"This is the only room I have that's available. It's clean, and the bathroom is just down the hall." He pointed.

"How much?"

The old man told me the price. "Are you working?"

"No. I used to own a jazz club, but it was destroyed in the bombing."

The old man nodded.

I imagined he was wondering how I would pay for the room without a job. "I do have some savings. It should last until I find work."

We stood in silence for a moment before the old man finally spoke. "Would you like the room?"

"I think so," I said.

"Do you have any bags or clothes you need to move in?"

"No. I'm afraid I've lost everything."

The old man nodded again. He turned, and I followed him back down the stairs.

"This is where I live." He opened the door I had seen earlier on the first floor. "Come in."

I followed him into the apartment, which was clean and organized.

"I'll be right back," the old man said.

I stood in the living room waiting for him to return. On the table next to the couch was a photo of an older woman.

"That's my wife," he said when he returned. "She was killed during the bombing."

"I'm sorry," I said.

"Your wife was killed too, wasn't she?"

"Yes. During the Blitz."

The old man again nodded. He was holding a small cardboard box. "I thought you could use some of these things. There's a bar of soap, a comb, some socks, a few other things."

"Thank you," I said. "That's very kind of you."

"My son is with the Pay Corp, and they're looking for some people to help clean up the debris from the bombing. I thought you might…"

"Yes, I would be interested," I said.

The old man handed me the key to my room, then wrote out his son's name and address on a piece of paper and handed it to me. "If you need anything…"

"Thank you," I said. The man's generosity made me uncomfortable. I wasn't used to being in a position of need, and despite the man's kindness, I didn't like it.

"I think I'd like to lie down now." I excused myself from the old man's apartment and walked silently to my new home.

Chapter 39
(1941)

I must have been exhausted because when I laid down in my room, I slept until the sun woke me the next morning. I felt refreshed, but hungry, so I set out to get my day started.

At Coddington's, a small diner nearby, I ordered poached eggs on toast. The previous day I had paid a month's rent on my room, which didn't leave much money in my pocket. I would have liked a larger breakfast, but I didn't dare spend more money than necessary.

Next, I went to the bank to check on my personal accounts. I had a bit more money than I had expected. It wasn't much, but I knew it was enough to hold me over for a short time. The money for The Blue Note was in a different bank, so I made my way there next.

The day was cool, and I did not have a coat. I already knew I was going to have to buy at least one new shirt and a pair of pants I could wear while looking for a job. A coat was not in the budget.

At The Blue Note, Jeffrey and I would go over the accounts once each month. He oversaw most of the bills, so it was important we were on the same page when it came to our budget and account balances. The problem was, I had been out of commission for several months and had not spoken to Jeffrey. I didn't know if he was dead or alive, and I had no idea what had become of the money in my business account.

Although my wounded leg was pain-free, it was not as strong as it had once been. After walking several blocks, I had to stop and rest. It was going to take some time to build my stamina back.

While I kept moving—from the boarding house to breakfast, and from breakfast to the bank—I stayed focused on the task at hand. But when I stopped to rest, my mind immediately went to Kimberly and Jimmy. I tried to shoo the thoughts away, to think of something else, but my mind would not cooperate. I missed them both so much and I had no idea what my life would look like without them in it.

I had not rested much, but I needed to get moving again to keep the thoughts of death and doom at bay. I began walking and my thoughts again turned to making it to the bank.

At the bank door, I stopped to catch my breath. I was a bit lightheaded, and I wanted to gather my thoughts before meeting with the bank manager. When I had composed myself, I went inside.

"May I help you?" the woman at the front desk asked. She wore a print dress with red flowers on it. The dress took my thoughts to our garden, the way it had been before the war.

"Can I speak with Graham Bentley?" I asked.

"Of course," she said. Can I tell him who is here to see him."

I gave her my name and while I waited, I looked around the lobby of the bank. Except for the posters advertising the sale of war bonds, it was business as usual. It would have been easy to assume that the people in the bank had not been impacted by the war. They simply went about their business, seemingly without a care about Hitler and his assault on the world. But I knew better. I knew that every person in the bank, every person in England, had been impacted one way or the other by the war.

"Mr. Ross." Graham offered his hand. "It's good to see you again."

I had not seen Graham in a year, maybe two. And even then, I had only met him a couple of times. I doubted he actually remembered me. Even so, he acted like I was a long-lost friend. He invited me into his office and offered me a seat. "How are you faring in these troubled times," he asked.

"As well as can be expected," I said. I saw no reason to tell him about Kimberly and Jimmy.

"I think we all are," he said. "Is that new?" he asked pointing to my eye patch.

I never thought about my missing eye until someone brought it up. I knew some people avoided talking about it for fear they would insult me. But the truth was, I appreciated the candor and curiousness it took to ask. "It is," I said. "From the bombing."

"Ah, The Blitz. Nasty business, that."

"It was. In fact, the bombs destroyed my business. Wiped out the building."

"I'm sorry to hear that," he said. "Are you looking for a loan to rebuild?"

"No, at least not now. I just wanted to get my account balance and a record of the last few months' transactions." I explained that I had been in and out of hospital for the previous few months and that I hadn't had contact with the manager of The Blue Note.

"That's easy enough," he said. "Give me a few minutes and I'll retrieve the information for you." Graham stood from his desk and left the office.

I honestly did not know what to expect. Jeffrey had always been loyal, but with The Blue Note gone and him unable to find me for months, I wondered if he had simply taken the money for himself. Part of me couldn't even blame him, especially if he was in dire need. After all, if he survived, he was going to need money, especially since he no longer had a job at The Blue Note.

Graham returned a few minutes later and handed me four sheets of paper. "Here are your last four months bank statements. If you need more, I can get them for you."

I took a moment to look over the statements. Four months earlier, Jeffrey had made several payments out of the account for rent, supplies, and payroll. Three months earlier, the payments stopped. Two months earlier, Jeffrey withdrew all but fifty pounds of the account balance.

"Is everything in order," Graham asked.

I stared at the bank statement, unsure what to make of it. "I'm not sure. It's looks like…I mean, I thought there'd be more money in the account."

"I see." Graham tilted his head. "Do you suspect foul play?"

Jeffrey had withdrawn more than three thousand pounds. Even so, I couldn't believe he had stolen the money. He must have thought I was dead. He knew The Blue Note had been destroyed. If he had tried to track me down, he would have learned that my home was ruins and I was nowhere to be found. If I had been in his shoes, what would I have thought?

I cleared my throat. "No, not foul play. Just a surprise."

I withdrew twenty pounds from the account to make sure I could meet my daily expenses.

I had a new task. I needed to find out what happened to Jeffrey. I had never been to his home, but I knew he rented a place on Groombridge Road in Hackney, near Wells Street Commons. He spoke about it often. It was too far away to walk, so I hailed a taxi outside the bank.

The going was slow. Debris from the bombings still littered many streets, and we had to turn around a few times to make our way out to Hackney. When we got there, my heart sank. The area had been destroyed by German bombs. Very few houses were left, and those that were, had some level of damage.

"Is this where you want to go," the taxi driver asked.

I had no idea which house was Jeffrey's. Considering how much damage there was, it was unlikely his house had survived. I was about to tell the taxi driver to take me back home when I noticed an old lady out in her garden picking up debris. "Wait here," I told the taxi driver. "I'll be right back."

I walked toward the old woman. She stood in front of one of the few homes that had sustained relatively little damage. She saw me coming toward her and shielded her eyes from the sun. "What do you want?" She held a brick in her hand.

"I'm looking for someone."

"They ain't here." The woman wore a heavy wool coat over a tattered dress that went to her ankles. She was stooped over, and her wispy white hair protruded from her head at strange angles.

I chuckled. "You don't know who I'm looking for yet," I said. "How can you be sure?"

She examined me for a moment without speaking. "What happened to your eye?"

I reached up and touched my patch. "The Blitz," I said.

"Are you American?

I nodded. "I am."

Her face seemed to brighten a bit. "And you was hurt in The Blitz?"

"I lost my eye and hurt my leg and ribs."

She nodded slowly. "I lost me Herbert in The Blitz," she said. "We was supposed to meet in the Underground, but he didn't make it."

"I lost my wife, too. We were on our way to the Underground."

"Bloody Germans," she said. "Who are you looking for?"

"Jeffrey Coe. Do you know him?"

She pointed across the street at a house that was now just a pile of rubble. "That was his house."

I stared at the house. No one could have survived the blast that did that kind of damage. "Is he dead?" I asked.

The old woman shook her head. "No, he and Millie went to be with her mum in Dublin before we got hit. I'm happy for Millie, but that Jeffrey is a cranky bastard."

I exhaled deeply and let out a laugh. "Yes, he is," I said. "Do you have an address for them in Dublin?"

"They didn't tell me, and I didn't ask."

I was relieved to learn that Jeffrey was alive, but that didn't get me any closer to my money. "Thank you for your help" I turned to walk away, but then had a thought. I turned back toward the old woman. "Who did you think I was when I walked up?"

"I thought you was one of those men from the landlord. I haven't been able to pay me rent since the bombs killed Herbert." Every time she mentioned Herbert, I expected her to cry. Instead, she was matter of fact, as if losing Herbert, who I assumed was her husband, was just another unfortunate fact of life during wartime.

I reached into my pocket and took out my wallet. Inside, was the twenty pounds I had just withdrawn from the bank. I took it out and handed it to the old woman. "This is for you. I hope it helps."

"Herbert didn't like taking charity," she said.

"I won't tell him if you won't." I winked.

She seemed to like that and stuffed the money in her coat pocket.

Chapter 40
(1941)

At the offices of the Royal Army Pay Corp, I told the woman at the front desk that I'd like to see Captain Anthony Beckley, the old man's son.

"Is he expecting you?" She pursed her lips.

"No, but his father sent me."

The receptionist did a double take. "I'll see if he's in."

I wore a new pair of black slacks and a white button-down shirt with an open collar. It had been twenty years since I looked for a job, and the prospect of being interviewed didn't excite me. I'm not sure why. How hard could an interview be for a job that involved picking up debris? Even so, I was not looking forward to answering questions.

A short, pale soldier in a khaki uniform entered the lobby. "Mr. Ross?" he asked.

I stood. "Captain Beckley?"

The soldier laughed. "No. I'm Corporal Evans. Will you follow me, please?"

I followed the soldier through a maze of offices and army personnel until we came to Captain Beckley's office. Corporal Evans knocked on the door and a voice from inside said, "Come in." We entered and Evans said, "Captain, this is Mr. Henry Ross."

"Thank you," the captain said. "That will be all." The corporal saluted, then left the office, closing the door behind him.

"Mr. Ross, please have a seat." The captain motioned to a chair across from his desk. "I'm glad you came in." The captain was tall and thin, with an angular face and a receding hairline. I guessed him to be in his mid-to-late thirties.

"Thank you for seeing me," I said.

"Let me get right to the point. The British Army has charged me with cleaning up the mess made when the Krauts dropped their bombs on our fair city. We dug right in and we're cleaning up the mess, but now they want to take away my corporal, send him to the front, and leave me without an assistant. Something about having our fighting men actually out fighting. Can you imagine?" The captain smiled. "So, I am forced to hire a civilian to take on the job Evans has been doing.

I assumed that any job I might get would involve actually cleaning up debris around the city. "I see," I said, not sure what else to say.

"My father tells me that you used to own The Blue Note."

"Yes, that's right."

"I know it well," he said. "I've been there several times. I saw Duke Ellington there once. He was wonderful."

"You're a jazz fan?" I asked.

"I'm not an aficionado, but I enjoy the music," he said.

I nodded. I had the urge to turn our conversation toward jazz, but thought better of it.

"So, I don't want to waste a lot of time looking for someone to replace Evans. Would you like the job?"

I was taken by surprise. Our short conversation had not really been a proper interview. Even so, I jumped at the opportunity. "Yes, I would like the job."

"Very well." The captain stood and offered his hand. "Can you start tomorrow?"

"Of course, tomorrow would be fine."

Chapter 41
(1941)

I got into the habit of going for a pint or two after work to the Lion's Head Pub with a couple of chaps from the Royal Army Pay Corp. I enjoyed the company, and the alcohol helped me sleep at night. Without it, my mind ran wild with thoughts of Kimberly and Jimmy. If I allowed it, the thoughts would keep me up all night.

Once or twice a week, I'd play piano at the Lion's Head. The owner, Rupert Manly, paid me in drinks. In a short time, I developed a bit of a following, and when I was scheduled to play, the place filled up. That made old Rupe a happy man.

On a cold Sunday night in early December, a good crowd gathered to listen to me play. Spirits were high. One of the regulars requested I play the "Maple Leaf Rag" by Scott Joplin. The song reminded me of Sally, and the thought made me wistful. When I finished, the patrons gave me a standing ovation.

One person yelled, "Another masterpiece from the Piano Playing Pirate." They had taken to calling me this because of my eye patch. I didn't mind. I viewed it as a term of endearment.

"Play another one, Pirate," another person said.

The recognition felt good. I had a group of good people in my life, even if it was just for a few hours a couple times a week. It was a welcome distraction.

I was about to play another song when Rupert yelled out from behind the bar.

"Wait a minute, Henry. Wait. Listen to this." He turned on the radio that sat behind the bar and turned the volume up. Everyone became quiet.

"…to Bob Trout for the report." There was a bit of static, then an American voice came over the radio.

"This is Bob Trout reporting from London where Prime Minister Winston Churchill and the British Parliament just met in special session to receive the news that the US naval base in Pearl Harbor, Hawaii was attacked today by Japanese air forces. The attack did considerable damage to America's Pacific Fleet, as well as to the area around the naval base, including the city of Honolulu. We have not received an official number of casualties, but our reporters in Hawaii have been told it is in the hundreds."

The report went on, but I was lost in my thoughts.

When the report concluded, Rupe turned the radio off. "Looks like the Yanks are going to be drawn into the war after all."

"What do you think, Pirate? Do you think the Yanks are going to help us fight the Germans?"

I had not lived in the United States for more than twenty years. I knew much more about what England was doing than I did about what America was going to do. Even so, I didn't see any way they could stay out of the fight now.

"I don't know, mates," I said. "But I think the Japs just woke up a sleeping giant."

The crowd cheered.

The day after the attack, the U.S. declared war on Japan, and a few days later, Germany declared war on the U.S. The Americans were coming to Europe to fight Hitler and the Third Reich. Hopes were high in England that, with the U.S. involved in the war, Germany would be quickly defeated. But nearly two months passed before U.S. troops arrived in large numbers in England. In the meantime, Hitler continued his ground assault across the continent. Nightly bombings in London during The Blitz had ceased a few months earlier, but England continued to be in peril from Germany and their Axis partners.

At work, our days were busy and hectic. There was so much to do, and now that the Americans had arrived in England, we were being pulled in even more directions. Captain Beckley handled the stress with grace and good humor. His composure helped the rest of us to stay calm and do our jobs.

I popped my head into his office one evening to say good night, and he motioned for me to come in and have a seat.

"Another long day," he said.

I laughed and agreed. It seemed like all our days had been long ones.

"I appreciate the work you're doing here, Henry. It makes my job much easier."

"Thank you," I said. "It's good to be able to help."

"I've never asked you about your personal life," Beckley said. My father told me that your wife was killed in The Blitz."

"That's right," I said. It had been months since she died, but it was still not easy to talk about Kimberly's death.

"My mother died during the bombings, too."

I nodded. We sat in silence for a few moments.

Beckley cleared his throat. "Do you have any kids?"

I smiled and looked away. "We had one. A boy. He joined the RAF, was a pilot. He was shot down and killed."

"Oh, God. I'm sorry, Henry. I didn't know." Beckley seemed genuinely sorry for bringing up the subject.

"I used to be a furniture dealer," Beckley said. "When the war started, I closed down my shop to enlist. I thought I'd be back to re-open it in a few months, maybe a year. I was foolish enough to think we'd drive Hitler and those godless Huns back into Germany with no problem." He shook his head and laughed.

"I was at Dunkirk last year when we had to be evacuated by small private boats. I was on a sailboat meant for eight or ten people. We had thirty lads on the boat, plus the old man that owned it and his mate. And I felt bloody lucky to be on that boat. A lot of the lads didn't make it even that far."

He inhaled deeply and took a moment, seemingly trying to compose himself.

"When I got back to England, I was promoted to lieutenant." He pronounced the rank as lef-ten-ant, the way the English do. "I must have done something right, because just a few months later, I was promoted again to captain and assigned to the Pay Corp. Every day I sit at this desk, I feel both guilty and grateful. There's part of me that wants to be out there fighting Germans. But I've seen combat, and I'm thankful I'm here where the biggest danger is from paper cuts."

Beckley laughed and brushed some invisible dust from the top of his desk. "Even if we win this war, how can we ever live on the same planet with the Germans again. They've taken so much from us and done such horrible things. How are we supposed to ever forget that?"

I shrugged. "Isn't that always the way with war? Somebody wins, somebody loses, and to the victor go the spoils. I imagine we'll make it pretty rough on the Jerrys, assuming we win."

"You sound like a military man," he said. "Are you interested in enlisting?" Beckley laughed and pushed his chair away from the desk. "I think I'm going to go home and get good and proper soused."

That was my queue that our conversation was over, the longest conversation we had ever had.

I left the office not sure how I was going to spend my night. I knew the gang would be at the Lion's Head. They were there almost every night. But the truth was, I didn't feel much like company. Talking about Kimberly and Jimmy—even just a little bit—had put me in a melancholy mood. Perhaps Beckley was right. Maybe going home and getting proper drunk was the best course of action.

Chapter 42
(1942)

I settled into a much-needed routine: six days a week at the Pay Corps and nights either drinking at the Kings Head or drinking and feeling sorry for myself at home.

Before the war, I enjoyed a glass of wine or pint of Guiness now and again, but I never felt the need to drink. Now, as every night approached, I feared I wouldn't be able to sleep without a little liquid encouragement. And each morning, my head pounding from the previous night's imbibing, I swore to myself that there must be a better way. By the end of the day, not having found a better way, I turned once again to the bottle.

There were plenty of people—mostly men—who turned to drink to help them cope with the war. They had lost loved ones, homes, and jobs. Some were simply scared, with the world at war and them stuck at home unable to do anything about it.

One night, three of us sat around a table at the Kings Head. Donnie Hathaway was a red-faced lad about ten years my junior. Claude Ferell was an old man, maybe sixty-five or seventy, with wispy gray hair and a permanent frown.

"How are you going to fight with that bum leg," Claude asked Donnie, who had suggested he was going to join the Army. Donnie had been born with a withered leg, which made him walk with a pronounced limp.

"You don't need to be able to walk well to shoot a rifle," Donnie said.

"But you have to walk to get where you're going before you can shoot the rifle, you dim bulb."

"Bollocks. I'd be just fine."

I couldn't help but laugh. None of us were in any condition to join the fight. "Maybe we should just sit here, have another drink, and leave the fighting to others."

"I'll buy if you go up and get them," Claude said.

"I'll drink to that," Donnie said. "Cheers." He raised his glass and finished what little beer was left inside.

It was a slow night at the Kings Head. In addition to me, Donnie, and Claude, there were probably only six or seven other people in the pub. I ordered beers for the table, and when I got back, Freddie Pasco, a co-worker from the Pay Corps, had joined us. Freddie was a good sort, always friendly. He was also unusually short, not quite five feet tall. He didn't come to the pub often.

"Freddie, what brings you out tonight?" I set a Guinness each in front of Donnie and Claude, then took my seat.

"I wanted to see if you chaps knew any more about the fighting in the Philippines. I just heard that the Japanese took over the country."

"I thought the Americans were holding the Philippines," Donnie said.

"The Japs drove them out. I heard they took thousands of Americans prisoner."

"Bloody hell," Donnie said. "It's not looking good for the Yanks."

"Do you know any more, Henry?"

I shook my head. This was all news to me. If it was true, Donnie was right. It wasn't looking good for the Americans.

We sat around drinking our beers. Nobody spoke. We spent most of our time going about our business, believing the Allies would win the war and our lives would somehow go back to normal. Then, there would be news of a defeat or setback, and the harsh reality would slap us upside the head.

Freddie stood. "I'm heading back home to the missus. Sorry to be the bearer of bad news."

We said our goodbyes and Freddie walked out of the Kings Head. "I wish that short little bloke had kept the news to himself," Claude said.

I nodded, but knew it wasn't Freddie's fault. If we hadn't heard the news from him, we would have heard it from someone else. There was no escaping news of the war, especially if it was bad news. I pushed my chair away from the table. "I'm heading home too."

"It's still early," Donnie said.

He was right. It was early, but I didn't want to be out around people. I was going to need a couple more drinks before I'd be able to sleep, but I could do that at home, where no bad news could find me.

Chapter 43
(1943)

It was a beautiful spring evening in London. The skies were clear, and we had near-summer temperatures. People were in a good mood. News of the war had been good for a change. In February, Germany surrendered to Russia in Stalingrad, and Allied Naval Forces had defeated Germany, effectively ending the naval war in the Atlantic. Just a few days earlier, German and Italian forces surrendered in North Africa. The tide was turning.

I finished playing piano at the Lion's Head and was at the bar talking to Rupe, the owner of the pub.

"Good crowd tonight, Pirate. Maybe this damned fighting is almost over."

"I'm not getting my hopes up yet," I said. "The Krauts aren't going to just roll over."

"You're a cynical bloke, aren't you?" Rupe slid another pint in front of me. "Have another drink and try to be more positive."

Rupe walked down the bar to wait on a customer and I finished what was left of my old drink so I could concentrate on the new one. Because people were in such a good mood, they had been buying me beers all night while I played. I didn't need more beer, but I was not going to turn it down either.

"I like the way you play."

I turned to see a beautiful woman with long blond hair and big brown eyes. "What's that?" I asked.

"Your piano playing. I really like it."

"Thank you. I appreciate that."

"My name is Mindy Parsons," she said.

Early in the war, it was unusual to see a woman in a pub. Lately, it had been commonplace. I had to admit, I liked the change. I introduced myself and asked if I could buy her a drink. I was just being friendly, but I suddenly realized my gesture was also a bit of an unintended come on.

"Thank you, but I'm okay." Mindy held up her glass, which was nearly full. "Do you play here often?"

"A couple times a week. The owner is a friend. He pays me in drinks." I took a big swig of my Guiness. My head was swimming. I tried to focus my good eye on Mindy's face. Even through my blurry vision, I could see that Mindy was younger than me. I guessed her to be early to mid-thirties.

The pub was loud. A group of soldiers on leave were in the corner singing, and it was hard to hear what Mindy was saying.

"I'm sorry. What did you say?"

Mindy repeated herself, but all I caught was "…walking home."

I shook my head and pointed to my ear.

Mindy motioned for me to follow her, and we walked out the front door of the pub. Mindy left her drink on the bar, but I still carried my beer.

Outside, Mindy turned to me. "I was saying that the pub is too loud and crazy, and I asked if you'd walk me home."

"Oh." I took a slug of my Guiness. Why would this beautiful woman want an older guy like me with just one good eye to walk her home? Surely, she didn't have romantic intentions. Or did she? Did I have romantic intentions? Should I? "Sure, just let me…" I raised my glass, drained it, and walked back into the pub. I set the glass on the first table inside the door and returned to Mindy. "Okay, I'm ready." I sounded like an eager schoolboy.

As we walked, Mindy told me that she lost her husband three years earlier in North Africa. "He died in a Jeep accident," she said. "He didn't even get shot."

"I'm sorry," I said.

"Time passes, and you realize that life goes on," she said. "Trevor died. I didn't, and I have to keep living."

I nodded and grunted. I understood her words, but I wasn't sure if I agreed with them. Kimberly had been dead for three years, just like Trevor, but I was not ready to move on. I wasn't sure I ever would be.

Mindy stopped and turned toward me. Her voice was soft and sultry. "Do you know what I mean?"

Before I could say anything, Mindy leaned up and kissed me. It was gentle at first but became more insistent. I pulled her close and returned the kiss. She felt good in my arms.

She looked up at me, her hand on my cheek. She ran her thumb across my lips, then stepped back. "I live right over there." She pointed to a building across the street. She grabbed my hand and began leading me toward her home. After a step or two, I stopped.

"What's wrong?" she asked.

My head was spinning. I thought about Kimberly, the woman I still loved. "It was nice meeting you." I pulled my hand away from hers. "Have a good night."

I turned and walked toward home.

Chapter 44
(1943)

I was at my desk reviewing some paperwork when Gladys Higgins let me know I had a phone call. I didn't have a phone at my desk, so I had Gladys transfer the call to an empty desk with a phone.

The caller identified himself as Harold Conroy with the Empire & Eastern Insurance Company. "Mr. Ross, I'm calling in reference to the claim you filed on your home in Osterley."

I had finally gotten around to filing a claim with my insurance company. I should have filed it sooner, but I just couldn't bring myself to deal with the aftermath of everything that had happened "Yes, thank you for getting back to me."

He got right to the point. "I'm afraid I have some bad news for you," he said. "Your policy does not cover damage caused by acts of war."

I let his words sink in. "I don't understand. There's no coverage?"

"Your home was damaged during The Blitz, wasn't it?"

"Yes, it was destroyed by German bombs. Did you go out and look at it?"

"No. You see, there's no need to inspect the property because your policy does not cover damage caused by acts of war."

I drew in a deep breath and switched the telephone receiver to my opposite ear. "You mean, all of the homes, all of the people who lost everything in The Blitz don't have insurance coverage?"

He paused a moment. "I'm afraid that's correct."

"How are people supposed to repair their homes?" My voice rose. "What am I supposed to do?"

"I understand your frustration," he said. "The government is said to be putting a program together to help people in your situation, but I'm afraid there's nothing in place at the moment."

I couldn't believe what I was hearing. I was counting on the insurance money to help me make ends meet. Truth was, I didn't want to rebuild the Osterley house. With Kimberly and Jimmy gone, I no longer had a family or a need for our family home. But I needed the insurance money to live on. Financially, I was keeping my head above water. But I feared what would happen when the war ended, and all the soldiers returned home. I wasn't sure how long my job at the Pay Corp would last.

"Mr. Ross, are you still there?"

I hung up and stared at the wall. We paid our insurance bill for more than twenty years, never once making a claim. It didn't seem right.

When I returned to my desk, Freddie Pasco was dropping off more paperwork. "What's wrong with you, mate? You look like someone walked over your grave."

I told Freddie about my conversation with the insurance company. "What the hell am I supposed to do now?"

"I heard Churchill is going to set up a program to rebuild, but they say it isn't going to happen until the war is over."

"I can't wait that long."

Freddie shrugged. "Sorry, mate."

I sat back in my chair and let out a deep breath. Panicking was useless. I needed a plan for no matter what happened. If Germany won the war, I'd need money to get out of England and go to a more friendly country. Even if the Allies won, I'd need money to keep food on the table and a roof over my head until I figured out what to do with my life. It was time to start planning for the future.

Chapter 45
(1943)

Reginald Harris and I stood in the driveway of what used to be my home and looked at the sad sight. I borrowed a car to meet Reginald with the intention of selling him what was left of my property.

"Those Kraut's really did a number on us, didn't they, mate?" Reginald asked. "I see damage like this all over this area."

"They did," I said, not wanting to have an extended conversation with this man. "What can you offer me for it?"

"It's a nice lot in a good area, but the house is beyond repair and it's going to take a fair bit to demolish it and get it out of here." Reginald rubbed his chin and pursed his lips. "I could give you a hundred pounds for it."

A hundred pounds was an insult, but it was just about what I was expecting. Speculators like Reginald had been popping up all over the London area buying property on the cheap when people were desperate, hoping that when the war ended, they could sell the properties and make a fortune.

"A hundred pounds? The lot alone is worth six or eight hundred pounds. And I think the house can be repaired." Exposed to the elements for all this time, the house had gone downhill since the last time I saw it. I wasn't sure if anything could be done to save it.

Reginald eyed me and nodded his head. He seemed to appreciate that I was negotiating. "I could come up a little. What do you say to a hundred-and-twenty-five?"

"I say you're still too low. Let's do three hundred pounds."

"Oh, matey, that's too much. I couldn't go that high."

"What's the best you can do, Reginald? Let's stop this back and forth and give me your best offer."

Reginald smiled. He was a man who loved his work. "For you, because I like you, I'll go one-hundred-forty…No, no. One-hundred-fifty. That's the best I can do. My partners won't be happy, but I'll do that for you."

The offer was pathetic and an insult. Yet, I was happy to have it. I extended my hand. "We've got a deal."

***

With a hundred-and-fifty pounds in my pocket, my next stop was Westminster Bank near the Pay Corps offices. That was where the money Kimberly got from her parents had been kept all these years.

I met with a distinguished-looking man named Lionel Darby, the bank's senior vice-president. He was tall and thin, with a head full of gray hair that was parted on the side and swept back.

"I'm very familiar with the account you speak of," Darby said. "In fact, I worked with Kimberly's parents when I first started with the bank. I helped them set up the trust account for your wife."

"As I mentioned, she was killed during The Blitz, and, although I never wanted to touch the account, I find myself in need of some funds."

"I see," he said. "I don't mean to sound impertinent, but might you have any proof of your marriage to Kimberly and her unfortunate death?"

I pulled a manila envelope out of the leather-bound notebook I carried with me, undid the clasp, and pulled out copies of our marriage certificate and Kimberly's death certificate. "I think you'll find these in order." I slid the documents across the desk to Mr. Darby.

He studied the documents for a moment. As he did, his brow furrowed. "Mr. Ross, would you excuse me for a moment." Darby stood and walked out of his office.

I felt like a student who had done something wrong, and the teacher was going to fetch the headmaster. But for the life of me, I could not imagine what I had done wrong. I had to remind myself that the money belonged to Kimberly, and with her gone, it now belonged to me.

When Darby returned, he had another man with him that he introduced as Chauncy Briggs, the bank's assistant general solicitor. Briggs was younger and shorter than Darby, with a receding hairline, but equally formal demeanor.

"Mr. Darby told me why you're here, Mr. Ross. Let me extend my condolences on the death of your wife."

"Thank you," I said, trying to figure out the need for a solicitor.

"I'm afraid that we have an unfortunate and, frankly, embarrassing situation." Darby took his place behind his desk and Briggs sat in the chair next to me.

"Unfortunate and embarrassing?" I asked.

"Yes, you see, Malcolm Kline, Kimberly's brother, came into the bank a couple of years ago with his solicitor. Of course, we knew Malcolm and had done business with the Kline family for decades." Briggs cleared his throat and nervously adjusted himself in his chair. "Malcolm's solicitor provided us with a death certificate for Kimberly and represented Malcolm as her next of kin. The solicitor indicated that Malcolm wished to withdraw all of Kimberly's funds so he could deposit them into his account."

"And you gave Kimberly's money to him," I said.

"Yes, that's right."

"Unfortunate and embarrassing," I repeated.

Darby and Briggs both looked like they had gotten caught pilfering a cookie from the cookie jar.

"This can't be that hard. You gave the money to the wrong person. Just get it back and give it to the right person." Even as I said the words, I knew it was unlikely they would simply get the money from Malcolm and give it to me.

Darby spoke up. "Malcolm Kline is not the kind to part with money easily."

"I truly am sorry," Briggs said.

"What do you mean, 'you're sorry?' You took money that belongs to me, and you gave it to somebody else. Someone who lied to you to get it." I grew increasingly loud and angry. "You can't possibly expect me to simply accept your apology and walk out of here empty-handed."

Briggs held up his hands to calm me. His brow glistened with sweat. "I'm going to need to look into the matter further. We'll let you know what we find out just as soon as we can. But I'm afraid we can't do anything for you right now."

"I do apologize," Darby said.

I looked back and forth between the two men. When I arrived at the bank, I was reluctant to take out any of Kimberly's money. Now, I wanted every penny of it. It belonged to me, not her crooked brother. I stood and spoke in a low, but urgent voice. "I expect this to be made right, and I expect it to be made right quickly." Before either man could respond, I walked out.

Chapter 46
(1943)

I was playing at the Lion's Head when I saw Mindy across the room. I had not seen her in the month or so since the night I left her in the middle of the road outside her house. She was at a table in the corner, opposite the bar, and she looked as beautiful as ever.

Rather than drink her cocktail, she mostly just stirred it with a straw. Twice while I played, I saw two different men approach her. Twice, she shooed the men away.

I wasn't sorry for leaving Mindy the night I walked her home, but I was embarrassed. It was juvenile. In her mind, I must have seemed like a frightened child. Yet, here she was, back at the Lion's Head watching me play.

When I finished my set, Rupert met me at the piano with a beer. "You have a visitor, mate," he said and handed me the beer. He motioned with his head at Mindy. "That bird in the corner asked that I have you come see her." Rupert raised his eyebrows, mocking me.

"Thanks, Rupe."

I took my beer to Mindy's table. "Hello, Mindy."

"Hello yourself," she said. "Long time no see."

"How are you?" I took a slug of my beer.

"I'm hurt, Henry. A man walked me home then left me standing in the middle of the road." Mindy feigned being hurt, pouting, but could not hold back a smile.

"Yeah, about that…"

"Are you going to sit?" she motioned to the chair across from her.

"Thanks." I sat, took another drink of my beer, and leaned my arms on the table. "Let me explain what happened that night."

"I think I already know."

"What do you know?" I asked.

Mindy stirred her nearly full drink. "I know your wife died around the same time Trevor did. Why didn't you tell me?"

Mindy must have been checking on me, trying to figure out what was going on. "I guess I wasn't in a very talkative mood that night."

"Are you in a talkative mood now?"

I took a drink of my beer and studied her. "I suppose. What would you like to know."

Mindy tilted her head. "What happened to your eye?"

I had grown so used to having one good eye and wearing an eye patch over the other one, I usually didn't think much about it. When Mindy mentioned it, I reached up reflexively and touched my patch. "I lost it during the bombing," I said. "The same night Kimberly, my wife, was killed."

Mindy nodded slowly. "Do you still love her?"

"I do."

"Even after all this time?"

I finished my beer and set the glass on the table. I rotated it in my hands while I thought about Mindy's question. "During the day, I keep thinking about things I want to tell her. At night, I expect her to walk into the room."

"Maybe you haven't accepted that she's dead yet."

I wanted to disagree with Mindy, but I knew she could be right. "Could be," I said.

Mindy looked down at her still full drink. "It's hard, isn't it? To lose someone. One minute you're together and in love. The next they're gone, and you're left all alone."

"It is tough."

Mindy moved her gaze from her drink to my face. "That's why you have to move on, Henry. Even if you can't get over it. You still have to get on with your life."

I nodded, even though I wasn't sure I agreed with her. I wanted to get on with my life. I wanted it desperately. But between the war and my lingering feelings for Kimberly, that didn't seem to be in the cards. "I guess I'm not ready yet."

"Maybe going through the motions will help you be ready. Know what I mean?"

I knew what she meant, and I wondered if she was right. Maybe I'd never be truly ready, but that didn't mean I couldn't act like I was. Maybe it was the acting that led to truly being ready to move on.

"I think I do," I said. "What do you have in mind?"

"You could walk me home again. Maybe this time we'll get all the way across the street." She smiled.

I finished my beer. I tried not to think too hard about what I was about to do. I stood. "If you're ready, I am."

Chapter 47
(1943)

I woke up and was disoriented. It took me a second to remember the previous night. I was in Mindy's bed, alone.

I had forced myself to sleep with Mindy. She had convinced me that doing so would help me move forward with my life, but all it did was make me feel guilty. I cursed myself for the effort.

I heard sobbing coming from the living room, so I put on my pants and went to investigate. I found Mindy sitting on the couch, her head in her hands, and her shoulders heaving with each sob.

"What's wrong?" I asked.

The sound of my voice startled her. It took a moment, but she got her crying under control. "Oh, Henry, I'm so sorry. I thought I was ready."

I sat next to her and wrapped my arm around her. "Are you feeling guilty?"

She nodded.

"Me too."

We sat quietly for several minutes in the dark of her living room.

"Each day when I wake up, I think, this is going to be the day I move on. This is going to be the day my life moves forward. But it never is."

Mindy had stopped crying now and was leaning against me, her head on my chest. I stroked her long blonde hair. "I assume it will happen for both of us, someday. Unfortunately, today doesn't seem to be that day."

She laughed. "No, I guess not." She sat up and looked at me. "I'm trying to put Trevor in the past. To make him into someone I used to know, but it never works. He's still with me. Everywhere I go, everything I do, he's still there."

"You still love him, don't you?"

"I try not to, but yes, I do."

"I know it's been three years for both of us, but I think we need more time. I don't know how much, just more."

She nodded. "This was nice tonight. I'm glad it was you I made a mistake with. You understand."

I laughed. "Yes, it was nice making a mistake with you too."

We had run out of conversation, and I suddenly felt uncomfortable, like I was somewhere I didn't belong. I stood. "I'm going to get dressed," I said. "I should probably head home."

She looked up at me from the couch and nodded.

I returned to the bedroom, found my clothes, and got dressed. When I returned to the living room, Mindy had fallen asleep. I kissed her forehead and walked out into the night.

Chapter 48
(1943)

George Kirby-Cole was eighty-two years old, had white hair, stooped shoulders, round glasses that were connected to a chain around his neck, and he was utterly brilliant. Rupert had referred me to his solicitor, and his solicitor, who was too busy to take my case, referred me to George.

George was retired. He had been for more than five years. And he was bored. Rupert's solicitor told me George had been one of the top barristers in London in his younger days, and he needed something to keep him busy, something he could sink his teeth into.

When I arrived at George's large, beautiful estate, he met me at the front door wearing an expensive blue suit with a striking red tie. He led me to his library, where he had a desk at one end of the room and two chairs set in front of a large bookshelf filled with leather-bound law books. On a table between the chairs were two cups, saucers, and a pot of tea.

As I sat, he asked, "Would you like tea," I said I would, and he poured the tea into each of the two cups. His hands were strong and steady.

"Milk or sugar?"

"A splash of milk and a cube of sugar," I said. "Thank you, George."

George nodded. Once the tea was prepared, he slid the cup and saucer across the table toward me, picked up his own cup and saucer, and sat back in his chair. His movements were practiced and precise. He was not in a rush. It occurred to me that this was all part of his process, which was exacting and intentional.

He slowly sipped his tea, tilted his head back for a moment as if considering something important, then turned his attention to me. "Tell me about your case."

I explained how Westchester Bank had wrongly given Kimberly's money to her brother, Malcolm. He listened intently, never interrupting my story. I told him about Darby and Briggs, how they seemed sheepish about having given the money to Malcolm, and how I had gotten angry with them.

After I finished, George sat with his head bowed, staring at his cup of tea. He stayed like that so long, I thought he might have fallen asleep. Then he raised his head, his eyes gleaming.

"You have a good case, my boy." His voice was strong and confident. "I know this Malcolm Kline character. Bit of a nasty bloke. He won't give up the money easily. But the bank, they're the ones who made the error and who were responsible for Kimberly's money. They're the ones we'll go after."

I didn't care who came up with Kimberly's money, just as long as it was returned to me.

"Do you have any questions before I get started?" George asked.

I did, but I was a little embarrassed to ask it. I had lived in England for more than twenty years, but I never understood why some people were called solicitors and others were called barristers. When I asked George, he had a ready answer.

"Solicitors are good chaps who mostly work in offices and push papers around. Barristers spend their time in court, trying cases and making law. I'm a barrister. I even have my own powdered wig." When George smiled, his whole face lit up. "You, my boy, need a barrister."

When I left his estate, I felt I was in good hands. He had the experience and the knowledge to do a good job. More importantly, he seemed to relish the opportunity to extract some money from the scoundrels at the bank. I looked forward to watching him work.

Chapter 49
(1944)

Captain Beckley called me into his office and motioned for me to take a seat. He pushed aside some papers he had been signing, then rested his hands on his desk.

"Have you noticed more Americans around town recently?"

"Now that you mention it, I have."

"What do you think it means?"

People around the Pay Corps—and at the pub, for that matter—always came to me with questions about Americans. It was an odd phenomenon. Truth was, I didn't have any idea why there had been more Americans in London recently. I shrugged. "Troop buildup, I suppose, but I don't know why they're here. Do you think something is going on?"

"Could be, but whatever it is, it's above my rank."

Beckley was a 'by the book' kind of guy, but once in a while, he liked to deal in a little wartime gossip. He was a good soldier, but underneath that starched uniform was the furniture dealer he had been before the war.

"I did hear that the Germans were pushed out of Russia and that the Allies have bombed German positions in Italy. Maybe the buildup has something to do with all of that."

Beckley considered my thoughts for a moment and nodded. "Could be. God, I wish I was out there."

"Do you really? Seems a lot safer here."

Beckley shrugged. "I don't know. When I was out there fighting, all I could think about was getting back home. Now that I'm home, I want to be out there fighting. Seems I just can't be happy." He laughed. "There are thousands, maybe millions, of guys out there that would love to be in my position. Seems odd for me to wish I was in theirs."

"Human nature, I suppose." I shrugged. "You know, the grass is always greener."

"I suppose. Of course, someone has to clean up the mess made by the Jerrys." We both laughed. "How is your claim coming against the bank?"

"We have a face-to-face meeting with the bank next week. I hope something gets resolved then."

"Did you ever find out how much money the bank cheated you out of?"

George spent the better part of three months trying to get the bank to confirm how much money Kimberly had in her trust fund. They were reticent to reveal the amount, but George got the court to force them to provide documentation of the account's value.

"The bank says there was just over forty-seven thousand pounds in the account."

"Yowza!" Beckley said. "That's worth fighting for."

I nodded.

"Once the war's over, maybe you can buy some new furniture from me. I'll give you a deal."

"That's kind of you," I said. "Maybe I can even get a place where I can put the furniture."

Beckley laughed. "Of course. First things first."

Chapter 50
(1944)

We were greeted at the bank by Chauncy Briggs, the solicitor I had met during my prior visit, and a serious-looking man named Calvin Finch, who was introduced as Westchester Bank's general solicitor. Both were well dressed and seemed to exude confidence. Along with the two men was a rather attractive young woman with reddish hair who neither man bothered to introduce.

"Barrister, I'm so pleased to see you," Finch said to George. "I heard you had died."

The young woman gasped slightly.

George took Finch's comment in stride. He chuckled. "Greatly exaggerated."

We took our seats around the bank's conference table. Briggs sat on the opposite side of the table from us along with Finch to his right. The young woman sat to Briggs' left. It wasn't clear initially what her purpose at the meeting was, other than to possibly distract us.

After a few pleasantries, George reiterated our demand that the bank provide us with all the funds they gave to Kimberly's brother.

Finch listened carefully but seemed unfazed by what George had said. "As we've said in the past, Malcolm Kline has the money that belongs to you. If you want to recover it, you'll need to bring him into the claim."

Since we started the process of trying to collect Kimberly's money, the bank had consistently maintained that we'd have to collect it from Malcolm. In a sense, I could understand their point. Malcolm had Kimberly's money, and it seemed only right that he should give it back. George looked at it differently. To George, the bank was the culprit in this story. They were entrusted with looking after Kimberly's money, and without conducting any due diligence, they simply handed it over to Malcolm.

"Ah, yes. Mr. Kline," George said. "I had the pleasure of talking to his solicitor, a lovely chap named Robert Gregg. Perhaps you met him when he accompanied Mr. Kline to your establishment."

Finch and Briggs looked at each other without saying anything, then turned their attention back to George.

"Solicitor Gregg tells me that Malcolm was not aware that his sister had married. As you may know, brother and sister were estranged. They had not spoken in many years. Isn't it sad when families fall apart? Sad business, that."

George waited for Finch and Briggs to agree with him.

"Yes, quite," Finch said.

Briggs nodded, his balding head glistening with sweat. He pulled a white handkerchief out of his back pants pocket and wiped his forehead.

"I am told that Mr. Kline provided you with a death certificate for his sister, is that correct?"

Finch looked at Briggs, as if urging him to answer.

Briggs rifled through his file, pulled out a paper, and slid it across the table to George. "Yes, of course. We would have never released the funds without the death certificate."

"Of course." George picked up the death certificate and studied it.

"As you can see, the death certificate does not list Mr. Ross as her spouse," Briggs said.

George slid Kimberly's death certificate back across the table to Briggs. "An unfortunate oversight. The night Kimberly died, my client was also injured. In fact, he was in hospital for months. Perhaps that's why the specialist judge didn't list Mr. Ross on the death certificate. I trust you consulted with him before releasing the funds to Mr. Kline." George told me during our previous meeting that the specialist judge was what we in the United States called a coroner.

Finch looked at Briggs again.

Briggs wiped his forehead with the handkerchief. "Well, no. No, we didn't. We already knew what he had indicated on the death certificate. It didn't seem necessary to talk to the specialist judge as well."

"I see," George said. "Seems necessary now, doesn't it?"

Briggs looked like he was going to get sick.

"Of course, you must have done some other due diligence to make certain that Mr. Kline was next of kin. You see, Solicitor Gregg told me that the day he and Mr. Kline came in to see you, he presented the death certificate, and you gave him a draft for the…" George pulled a paper out of his file and put his glasses on to read it. "…Forty-seven thousand two hundred-and twenty-seven-pounds sterling. Surely, he must be wrong. You wouldn't hand over more than forty-seven thousand pounds without doing some due diligence to determine if, in fact, Mr. Kline was entitled to that money, would you?"

Sweat dripped from Briggs' forehead. He breathed heavily as he wiped it away with his handkerchief. "No, you see, we had the death certificate showing that Kimberly Kline did not have a spouse. Mr. Kline represented to us that he was the next of kin. We knew Mr. Kline and valued his family's business with the bank over the years."

"Ah, yes. May I see the sworn statement you received from Mr. Kline indicating that he was the next of kin?"

Finch stared at Briggs and Briggs stared at George. Neither of the bank's men seemed to want to speak.

Throughout the meeting, the woman Finch and Briggs brought with them took notes. Now, as both men sat silently, she looked up from her notepad. For an instance, she smiled, then regained her composure and sat stoically, waiting for someone to speak.

It was Briggs who broke the silence. "As I said, we knew Mr. Kline. He had been a client before moving his business to Barclay's. We trusted him when he said he was next of kin."

"So, you don't have a sworn statement?" George asked.

Briggs shook his head. Sweat dripped down onto the table and he quickly wiped it away.

George sat ramrod straight in his chair. By contrast, Finch and Briggs slouched. Briggs had sunken so far down into his chair I thought he might disappear beneath the table.

George gathered his papers and returned them to the file. He put his hands flat on the table. "Gentlemen, I'm afraid you may have a bigger problem than what we've been discussing. I seriously doubt that your board will stand idly by when they hear that their counsel is giving away customers' money without proper documentation or due diligence. I haven't practiced law in some time, but I believe that's still referred to as malfeasance."

"I think we'd be better served concentrating on the issue at hand," Finch said.

"Perhaps you're right," George said. "What did you have in mind?"

"You've made your position clear," Finch said. "I appreciate you coming in today. Chauncey and I will need to discuss this further with the bank officers, and we'll get back to you just as soon as we can."

"Splendid." George stood. "Henry, let's leave these men to their work." He turned to Finch and Briggs, who were now standing. "Good day, gentlemen." He turned to the young woman. "Madame, it was a pleasure." The woman blushed and looked down at her notepad. George nodded to me, and we took our leave.

Chapter 51
(1944)

American soldiers began to disappear from London streets at the end of May and first few days of June. Everyone had a theory, but no one knew for sure what was happening.

"Something is up," Captain Beckley said. "There's too much troop movement for it to be just routine rotation of soldiers."

"A guy at the pub last night said he heard the Americans were pulling out to go home," I said. "He claimed the Americans have decided the Allies can't win the war, so they're going home and leaving England to the Germans."

Beckley shook his head and laughed. "Most of our best military intelligence comes from some drunkard who's half-pissed in a London pub."

His comment made me laugh too.

A couple days later, shortly after I arrived at work, Beckley called me into his office and had me shut the door. He had a radio on his desk, and an announcer was talking about a "special report."

"This is the BBC Home Service. And here is a special bulletin read by John Snagge:

"D-Day has come. Early this morning, the Allies began the assault on the northwestern face of Hitler's European forces. The first official news came just after half past nine when Supreme Headquarters of the Allied Expeditionary Force—usually called SHAPE from its initials—issued communique number one. This said, 'Under the command of General

Eisenhower, Allied naval forces, supported by strong air forces, began landing Allied Armies this morning on the northern coast of France."

The report went on to say that there were no details to share about the landing or the battle with the Germans. All we knew was that the day we had been preparing for was finally here.

"Let's hope this is the beginning of the end of this damned war," I said.

"Let's hope." Beckley had a serious look on his face. "God speed to all our brave boys."

I went for a walk after work. It was overcast and drizzling, but I wanted to be outside, to see the sights of London. I was excited that the Allies had landed in France and had taken the fight to the Germans, but I feared that if it didn't work, Hitler would unleash his forces on England, and the Germans would not let up until we had surrendered, or they had bombed us into oblivion.

The King was scheduled to give a radio address that night, so I went home and warmed a can of soup on the hotplate in my room. I had thought about going out to the pub to listen to the King's speech, but I really wasn't in the mood for company. Ever since I heard the D-Day invasion report in Beckley's office, my mood had turned sour. This should have been a time for optimism, but I feared the worst. If the invasion didn't drive Germany back on their heels, I was afraid we would lose the ability to ever win the war.

The radio announcer droned on waiting for the King to give his speech. Finally, he introduced the King. After a bit of static and a moment of silence, the King's voice came through the radio speaker.

"Four years ago, our Nation and Empire stood alone against an overwhelming enemy, with our backs to the wall. Tested as never before in our history, in God's providence we survived that test; the spirit of the people, resolute, dedicated, burned like a bright flame, lit surely from those unseen fires which nothing can quench.

"Now once more a supreme test has to be faced. This time, the challenge is not to fight to survive but to fight to win the final victory for the good cause…"

Listening to the King's speech, I couldn't help but think of life back in the United States. I wondered what they were doing tonight, how they had prepared for the D-Day invasion, and if they had the same fears as me.

The future of the world literally hinged on the actions being taken on those beaches in France.

I was not a man normally given to prayer. I had vowed years earlier that I would not pray to a God so cruel as to take my beautiful wife and son. But with the battle raging in France and so many good and decent souls on the line, I kneeled beside my bed and offered up a prayer for the troops fighting this great battle, and for the men leading the fight. And most of all, I prayed that our fight was righteous and our cause noble in the eyes of God, if indeed there was a God.

For the first time in a long time, I went to bed without the aid of alcohol. So, as long as I was praying, I asked God to let me sleep through the night.

Chapter 52
(1944)

A few days after the D-Day invasion, German bombs fell on England again. But they weren't the old-style bombs dropped from planes. They were missiles, fired from a safe distance away in France and Holland. The Germans called the missiles V1s, but we referred to them as "doodlebugs" or "buzz bombs," because of the distinctive buzzing sound they made. The Royal Air Force did a good job of intercepting most of the missiles, but about one-in-four got through. That was still too many. The only bright spot was that radar could track the incoming missiles and warn civilians to get to a safe place before the missile arrived.

Hundreds of buildings were destroyed, and thousands died during the bombardment. If the motivation for dropping doodlebugs on us was to weaken our resolve, it didn't work. I was amazed that after days on end of missile attacks, the Brits dusted themselves off and recommitted to the fight. It was a sight to behold.

Prior to D-Day, George worked to get Kimberly's money from the bank, but they were balking, delaying. Finch and Briggs had both been fired from Westchester Bank, and a man named Charles McGreevey now handled the case for Westchester. I had not spoken to George for a few months, and once the bombs started falling, it didn't seem like the right time. But when June turned to July, and July to August, and the missile attacks became somewhat routine, I decided to reach out to George.

"Hello, my boy." George's voice was weak and raspy. "How are you holding up with all these blasted doodlebugs dropping on us every night?"

I told George I was staying safe. "How are you doing?" I asked. "You don't sound too good."

"I'm afraid I caught a bit of a cold, and it's turned into pneumonia." George coughed, and the effort left him breathless.

"Are you okay?"

He took a moment to catch his breath. "I'm fine," he said. "In fact, I'm on the mend. I felt much worse a few days ago. And I have a wonderful nurse right here by my side making sure I drink plenty of liquids and get lots of rest. She's a tyrant, but she means well."

I heard a female voice giggle in the background.

"Don't worry, my boy. I'll be up and out of bed in no time, and then we'll get your money from the bank."

When George hung up, I couldn't help but think about his age. Pneumonia could be hard on the healthiest person. I worried what it could do to an eighty-two-year-old man.

In September, Germany started launching a new kind of missile at us. The V2 was supersonic, making it impossible for the authorities to warn residents when a missile was incoming. Death tolls increased, but Brits adjusted, going about their business, as if being attacked by missiles was just an inconvenience of everyday life.

George called me in late October to let me know he had set up a meeting with Charles McGreevey at Westchester Bank. "I couldn't pin him down sooner than early December," he said. "We're meeting at the bank on the fourth at ten o'clock."

George sounded much better than he had during our previous phone call. He sounded stronger and more robust. More like the old George. I told him I looked forward to seeing him at the bank, and we hung up. It was the last time I ever spoke to him.

Chapter 53
(1944-1945)

In late November, George was killed when a V2 missile struck his estate. Rupert's solicitor heard the news and passed it on to Rupert. Rupert passed it on to me.

George was a good man who loved his work so much that he continued to do it even after he retired. He was a friend and a role model. I wished for myself that when I was George's age, I would still be doing what I loved. For me, that would be playing piano.

I called McGreevy at Westchester Bank and told him about George's death. He was sympathetic, but unmoved. I immediately disliked the man. I told him I would be back in touch as soon as I employed another barrister.

Christmas was a sad affair. I sat at home by myself and had soup for Christmas dinner. I suppose I should have felt lucky. I had a roof over my head and food in my belly. Not everyone had even that. Just the same, I missed Kimberly and Jimmy. I missed them all the time, but the pain and heartache of their absence always seemed worse around the holidays.

At work, we would get the debris from German bombing cleaned up from one area only to have them bomb another area. Captain Beckley referred to it as job security, but I knew it frustrated him too. He wanted to make progress on the cleanup, not just tread water.

In early January of 1945, I met with a barrister named J.R. Ripperton. He was well-respected in the legal community, and he came highly recommended from a colleague at work. Ripperton's office was in a plush building near Parliament Square and Westminster Abbey.

He was a dapper dresser, wearing a stylish suit complete with a silk pocket square. His black hair was slicked back, with no hair out of place. He invited me into his office and directed me to a chair in front of his desk. He took his place in a much larger chair behind his desk. He wore a pinky ring, which he spun on his finger as we spoke.

"I met George one time. I can't remember exactly when, but it was several years ago. He was an old man even then." He laughed at his own joke. "The old boy just couldn't give up his practice, could he?"

I laid out the whole story for Ripperton. He listened to everything I had to say, spinning the ring on his pinky finger the entire time.

"I know McGreevy," he said. "He can be a shrewd operator. How much money are we talking about?"

I told him, and his eyes widened. He seemed to be doing calculations in his head.

Ripperton sat up in his chair and steeled himself, as if he was about to make a pronouncement. "I think old George was barking up the wrong tree. Malcolm Kline has your money. We should go after him, not the bank."

"But the bank made the mistake. They gave my money—Kimberly's money—to Malcolm without doing their due diligence. I think the bank should pay."

"Due diligence." Ripperton smirked. "You see, the bank relied on Malcolm's assurance that he was the next of kin and rightful heir to his sister's money. But he lied." Ripperton spoke slowly, as if I was a school child.

"Yes, but…" I stopped myself and took a deep breath. I shook my head. "Thank you for your time. I appreciate it."

Ripperton said nothing. I think he was shocked. I simply stood and walked out. He certainly was no George, and he definitely wasn't the guy I needed to help me.

Chapter 54
(1945)

The Nazis stopped shooting V2 cruise missiles into England the previous month. We weren't sure why, but it was a welcome relief not hearing explosions every night.

I was in my room listening to the radio one night when I heard a report about the Allied liberation of Belsen Concentration Camp. Thomas, one of the other boarders, was listening to the radio with me, and he had brought with him a couple bottles of Barclay Perkins Dark Lager. Thomas had once been a haberdasher, but there wasn't much call for fine men's clothing during the war, so he had gotten a job working in a warehouse. We were both tired but had gotten into the habit of talking and listening to the radio on nights when I didn't go out.

Thomas opened the two bottles of beer and handed one to me. We were drinking our beer and talking, when the music on the radio suddenly stopped and an announcer said the BBC was interrupting normal programming for a special report from Richard Dimblebly in Germany. Thomas and I looked at each other, then became quiet.

"I have just returned from the Belsen concentration camp where I drove slowly about the place in a Jeep with the chief doctor for the Second Army. I had waited a day before going to the camp so that I could be absolutely sure of the facts now available."

He went on to describe a macabre scene. Germany had imprisoned Jews, Gypsies, and other 'undesirables' in camps with inhumane conditions. Many had starved to death or had been consumed by disease. Others had been intentionally killed in gas chambers, shot as part of mass shootings, or were burned alive in ovens. The corpses were then stacked around the camp like cordwood waiting to be buried in huge mass graves or incinerated in large ovens.

The report was unlike anything I had ever heard. Thomas had his back to me, so he didn't see me wipe away tears as the reporter detailed the atrocities that had taken place. At one point, Thomas exclaimed, "Oh my God." The report went on, detailing one inhumane tragedy after another. I felt the same way as Thomas.

As the report became even more graphic, Thomas stood suddenly. "I've heard enough. I'm going to bed." He left my room without turning around. I knew how he felt. Hearing the details of what was happening to prisoners at the hands of the Nazis was heartbreaking and infuriating. I wanted to turn away, to spare myself the soul-crushing pain, but I felt that was too easy. If these people—these innocent multitudes—had to endure such horrible atrocities, I felt I should have the courage to listen to what they went through, to be a sort of witness to the horrors that had taken place.

I took a drink of my beer and re-focused on Richard Dimbleby's voice.

"Babies were born at Belsen, some of them shrunken, wizened little things that could not live because their mothers could not feed them.

"One woman, distraught to the point of madness, flung herself at a British soldier who was on guard in the camp on the night that it was reached by the 11th Armoured Division. She begged him to give her some milk for the tiny baby she held in her arms. She laid the mite on the ground, threw herself at the sentry's feet, and kissed his boots. And when, in his distress, he asked her to get up, she put her baby in his arms and ran off crying that she would find some milk for it because there was no milk in her breast. And when the soldier opened the bundle of rags to look at the child, he found it had been dead for days."

Tears streamed down my face. I reached over and switched the radio off. I had heard enough. I finished my beer, got undressed, and went to bed. I had no wish to be awake in such a cruel, inhumane world.

Chapter 55
(1945)

The radio report from Belsen Concentration Camp seemed to change the mood around London. Attitudes turned dark. People walked the streets with their heads down. It was like the news of the Nazi atrocities pulled a veil over the world, leaving people somber and reflective.

A few days after the report, Beckley called me into his office. I had just arrived at work, and I got the impression he had been waiting for me.

"Have you seen this?" He handed me a newspaper.

I opened the folded paper and across the top of the front page in large, bold type were the words "HITLER IS DEAD." It took a second for the words to sink in. "Is this true," I asked.

"As far as I know," Beckley said. "It's in all the newspapers. The evil bastard apparently shot himself."

"So, is the war over?" I was trying to make sense of the news.

"Their new Fuhrer, a bloke named Admiral Doenitz, says they're going to keep fighting."

Like a lot of people, I had it in my head that Germany had somehow been hypnotized by Hitler, and if he wasn't around, everything could go back to normal. But if Germany was going to keep fighting, even after Hitler's death, what did that say about the people of Germany? "I assumed they'd stop fighting if Hitler died."

"I guess I did too. Maybe it's just a matter of time until they give up."

We were silent for a moment, considering the consequences of Hitler death. He had been the face of the Nazi regime, of all the hatred and ugliness that it represented. Hitler's death was a great thing for the world. But what was next?

"I want to save that newspaper," Beckley said. "I think I'm going to frame it and hang it in my house."

I handed the paper back to Beckley. He folded it carefully and placed it in his desk drawer.

That night, I noticed a change in the people I was around. It was like the veil had been lifted and the more positive, hopeful attitudes had returned. Hitler's death had somehow brightened the darkness that the news from Belsen had brought. It was as if the Belsen news had drained us of our hope, but just a few days later, Hitler's death had restored it.

At Kings Head that night, there was a festive atmosphere. People were celebrating Hitler's death. It felt wrong to me to celebrate the death of any person, but it wasn't really Hitler's death that was being celebrated. It was a celebration of the death of something evil, something that did not belong and needed to be eradicated.

Donnie and Claude were at their usual table. They were celebrating and asked me to join them. Claude even bought another round so we could toast properly.

"To a speedy end to this bloody war," Claude proposed.

"Cheers."

We clinked our pints and drank our beers.

"Do you really think the war will end soon?" Donnie asked.

"It has to, doesn't it?" Claude said. "Without Hitler and his crazy vision, what do the Krauts have to fight for?"

"I hope you're right," I said. "But I'm not sure if Hitler was leading an unwilling people or if he was just a reflection of what they really wanted."

Claude had to think about that. "I think Hitler was like a mad genius, controlling the people. I can't imagine that all of Germany wanted what he's done to the world."

"You might be right," I said.

"I hope whoever found him put a stake through his heart, just to make sure he was really and truly dead," Donnie said.

I laughed. "Like a vampire?"

"Yeah. Maybe they should shoot him with a silver bullet, too." Donnie laughed, and when he did, he snorted like a pig.

"That's an attractive laugh," Claude said. "Hard to believe you're single."

That got us all laughing, and Donnie snorted even more.

"Enough Hitler talk," Claude said. "Have you found yourself a barrister yet?"

"Nothing new," I said. "I'm still looking, but I don't think I'm going to find anyone like George."

Claude nodded and drank his beer.

I had not thought much about Kimberly's money in the past few days. My mind had been occupied by other matters. But things had dragged on too long. I needed to press Westchester Bank to give me Kimberly's money before it was too late to do anything about it. I felt lost without George, but maybe he had set the path for me to recover the money. Maybe all I needed to do was follow that path.

I suddenly felt excited about contacting Charles McGreevy at the bank. Of course, it was too late in the day to do anything about it immediately, but I needed to do some thinking. I drained my beer and stood. "I'm heading home."

"You just got here," Donnie said.

"I know, but there's something I have to do."

"Give her our regards," Claude said.

Donnie began laughing again, and as I walked away, I heard him snort.

Chapter 56
(1945)

I made an appointment to meet with Charles McGreevey the following week. My confidence and excitement from the previous night had drained, and I knew I needed to get it back before our meeting.

I had just finished playing at Kings Head on a Sunday night and was getting ready to leave when Rupert called me over to the bar. The pub had emptied out, and there were only a handful of people left in the place.

"Have you heard the rumor?" Rupert asked.

"What rumor?"

"I heard from a friend that Germany has surrendered."

"What friend?" I asked. "Don't you think they'd announce it if it was true?"

"I'm just telling you what I heard," Rupert said.

"I hope it's true. But I wouldn't put any money on it."

The next morning at the office, I told Captain Beckley what I had heard.

"Ah yes, the famous barkeeper intelligence network." Beckley laughed. "If it's true, I'll likely be the last to know."

"You haven't heard anything?" I asked.

"Not a word. But if I do, you'll be the first to know." Beckley gave me a wink and I left the office.

That night at Kings Head, I was getting ready to play when Rupert began shouting.

"Everybody, be quiet. Shut the hell up. Listen to this." He turned on the radio sitting behind the bar. The sound of static filled the speaker for a moment, then it was replaced by the announcer's voice.

"…regular programming to bring you a very special announcement from the Ministry of Information."

Everyone in the bar had become quiet. I sat on my piano bench waiting for the announcement. There were a few seconds of silence, then another voice came out of the radio.

"The British High Command has authorized the following statement: In accordance with arrangements between the three great powers, tomorrow, Tuesday, May eighth, will be treated as Victory in Europe Day and will be regarded as a holiday."

"The war is over," one of the bar patrons said, although it was as much a question as a statement.

"It's over," another patron said.

"Yes, that's what he said," Rupert said. "The war is over. Drinks on the house."

A cheer went up from the crowd, and I couldn't help but join in the celebration, even though I wasn't certain that the announcement meant the war was really over. But if that's not what the announcement was saying, then what did it mean?

When I got to work on Tuesday, Beckley was in his office.

"What are you doing here?" Beckley asked. "Didn't you hear that today's a holiday?"

"I heard the announcement last night, and I drank like it was the end of the war, but I still haven't heard that the war has actually ended."

"Strange, isn't it?" Beckley said. "If the war is over, why don't they just say as much?"

"I'm just an American and don't understand all your mysterious British ways." I smiled. "I was hoping you could decipher last night's announcement for me."

"Damned if I know. I've been expecting to hear something ever since that broadcast last night, but no one above me is talking."

"Either way, if it's a holiday, why are you here?" I asked.

"The Army doesn't take holidays," Beckley said. "As far as I know, we're still fighting a war." He pulled out a bottle of Hennessey VS Cognac from his desk drawer and poured some into his coffee cup. "But I'm hedging my bets just in case."

We shared a toast, then Beckley chased me out of the office. "Go enjoy your holiday," he said.

I left the Royal Army Pay Corps offices and joined some of my co-workers at the Lion's Head. I had already imbibed several pints when Rupert turned the radio up. It took a few seconds for everyone to become quiet, but I immediately recognized the voice on the radio as Winston Churchill's.

"…and our friend, Admiral Doenitz, designated head of the German state, signed the act of unconditional surrender of all German land, sea, and air forces in Europe to the Allied Expeditionary Force, and simultaneously, to the Soviet High Command…"

Churchill kept talking, but the cheers from the people in the pub made it impossible to hear what else he had to say. The war in Europe was over.

The celebration and revelry spilled out into the streets. Huge bonfires were lit, and impromptu parades took place. I joined one of the parades that went down Piccadilly, across Green Park, to Buckingham Palace. The parade became a mass of people waiting for the King to appear. We waited over an hour before George VI came out onto the balcony of the palace along with the royal family and Churchill. They all waved, and the crowd cheered.

Despite the revelry, I thought of my wife and son, and how, after their deaths, the war had given me a routine, a sense of purpose. Now I would have to start over. Again.

The celebration continued throughout London. I walked back to my room and stayed there the rest of the night.

Chapter 57
(1945)

The next day at the Pay Corps, we didn't get much work done. Most people were hungover, and all anyone wanted to talk about was the end of the war and what came next. Everyone in England had put their lives on hold, waiting for the war to end. Now, everyone looked forward to moving on with their lives.

After work, I stopped at the market to get something for dinner. I rarely had food at the boarding house because we had very limited icebox space, and because I did not like to cook in my room on the hot plate.

I was trying to decide what to get for dinner when I heard a familiar voice call my name.

"Mr. Ross, is that you?"

I turned to see Chauncy Briggs staring back at me. He was pushing a shopping cart with a head of lettuce, two tomatoes, and a few other items inside.

"Mr. Briggs. It's nice to see you." I was being polite. It was awkward seeing him. After all, I was indirectly responsible for him losing his job.

"Please, call me Chauncy." He wore a pair of baggy dress slacks, and a sweater over a button-down shirt. He looked much more casual than he had the last time I saw him.

"Sure, Chauncy. Please call me Henry."

"Isn't it wonderful that the war is over?" he asked. "We were up all-night celebrating."

"Yes, it's wonderful. I'm excited to have the world get back to normal."

"Yes, quite," he said.

There was an awkward moment of silence which I felt obligated to fill. I said the first thing that came to my mind. "You know, Chauncy, I heard you were made redundant at the bank, and I just wanted to say how sorry I am. I feel badly about that." The words were out of my mouth before I could stop them. It was true. I did feel badly about him losing his job. That was never my nor George's intention. Even so, I didn't mean to blurt it out.

"Oh, that's quite alright. That wasn't your fault. The bank needed a scapegoat, and I was the lucky bugger they chose, along with poor old Finch. Besides, I've landed on my feet. I'm the director of the London Aid Society. We're an organization that helps war widows and orphans. Unlike the bank, it's very rewarding work."

"That's wonderful, Chauncy. I'm pleased you're doing well."

"Did you ever get Westchester to give you your money?" he asked.

"No, not yet," I said. "I have an appointment with Charles McGreevy in just a few days. I hope to conclude the matter then."

Chauncy nodded and seemed to be thinking. He looked around, as if someone might be listening, then leaned in toward me, talking low. "You didn't hear this from me, but when we mistakenly gave the money to your brother-in-law, it never crossed our minds that he might not be the next of kin. We knew the family and knew Malcolm was Kimberly's brother."

Chauncy cleared his throat and looked around again before continuing. "But the real reason we weren't concerned is because we were hoping to lure Malcolm's business back to the bank. He had recently taken his funds out of Westchester and had moved them to Barclays. We wanted that money back in our bank."

"Are you saying that it wasn't a simple oversight?" I asked, my voice low and conspiratorial. "In other words, you weren't concerned about who the next of kin was. You were using the money to buy back Malcolm's business."

"That's right. In fact, you might want to tell McGreevy that Malcolm and his solicitor both can confirm that Lionel Darby and I practically got down on our knees to beg Malcolm for his business. We knew that recovering his business would be a feather in our caps and would be rewarded by the bank. They had offered us a bonus if we could convince Malcolm to come back to Westchester." Chauncy chuckled, and his eyes brightened. "Instead of earning a bonus, I was made redundant."

His chuckle turned into a full-on laugh. I wanted to laugh along with him, but I really didn't see the humor in the situation. I forced a laugh just to play along.

"And you think this news will help me get Kimberly's money?"

Chauncy nodded his head. "It would not be good for the bank to go into court and have their greed exposed. I'm certain you could get affidavits from Malcolm and his solicitor as to the facts of our meeting. If need be, you could probably force an affidavit out of me as well." He winked knowingly.

"Thank you, Chauncy," I said. "It's very decent of you to share this information with me."

"I didn't share it with you," he said, winking again. "A little birdie told you."

Chapter 58
(1945)

McGreevy sat behind his desk, doing his best to be tolerant of our meeting, but failing miserably.

"Mr. Ross, we've been over this several times." The exasperation was thick in his voice. "While we regret that we made an honest error distributing your wife's funds to her brother, if you want to recover them, you really need to talk to Mr. Kline. He has the money now."

"In fact, I have talked to him," I said. That wasn't true, but so far, being completely honest had not gotten me what I wanted. "He and his solicitor both tell me that your employees, Lionel Darby and Chauncy Briggs, didn't conduct any due diligence to confirm that he was my wife's legal next of kin. Instead, they happily handed the money over to him in hopes that he would deposit the money in your bank."

McGreevy's brow furrowed and he squirmed uncomfortably in his chair. I could tell I was striking a nerve.

"In fact, Malcolm advised me that he had moved all of his money—a considerable sum I would think—out of your bank not too long before claiming Kimberly's money. Darby and Briggs practically begged him to bring the money back to Westchester."

McGreevy reached into a gold-colored box on his desk and pulled out a cigarette. He lit it with a lighter that sat next to the box, inhaled the smoke, held it for a moment, then exhaled. "I think Malcolm and his solicitor misunderstand what happened that day. We do not beg customers to deposit their money with us."

"Perhaps I'm misinformed," I said, knowing full well I was not. "I'm under the impression that the bank actually offered Darby and Briggs a bonus if they could win back Malcolm's business. Is that not correct?"

McGreevy puffed his cigarette and slowly tapped the ashes into an ashtray, as if he was trying to buy time.

"A bonus? That doesn't sound like something Westchester would do."

"Are you saying there was no bonus offered to Darby and Briggs?" I asked. "Because we could certainly put them both under oath and question them."

McGreevy took one last drag of his cigarette and stubbed it out in the ashtray. He sat back in his chair. His shoulders relaxed and he exhaled. "Yes, I suppose you could." He looked up at the ceiling and seemed to be thinking. "This matter has dragged on for some time, causing us both a considerable amount of consternation. Perhaps we can bring it to a close with a payment of ten thousand pounds."

I knew I had him. But they owed me every penny of Kimberly's money. Of course, I also knew that to get every penny, I would have to hire a barrister and maybe even go to court. If I could end this today and walk away, I would be able to start thinking about the future instead of the past.

"I'd like to bring this to a close as well. But you're going to have to give me at least half of Kimberly's money. Twenty-five thousand pounds."

"That's more than half, Mr. Ross." McGreevy said quickly.

"I know, but I like round numbers. Twenty-five thousand and we can be done with this today."

"And you'll sign a release?"

"For twenty-five thousand, I'll sign. One pence less than twenty-five thousand and we go to court." I was feeling my oats. I knew I was in the right, and I refused to back down. McGreevy knew I was holding most of the cards. He dropped the indifferent act and smiled.

"We have a deal."

Chapter 59
(1945)

I said goodbye to Beckley on my final day at the Pay Corps. He had
been a lifeline at a time when I badly needed one, and I was grateful to him.
I thought of all the people I had not said goodbye to. Claude and Donnie
and Freddie had no idea what had become of me. Neither did Mindy
Parsons or Dr. Chambers. I was not good at goodbyes, so I avoided them
whenever possible.

The taxi pulled away from the Pay Corps and I directed the driver to an
address on Commercial Street, near the Aldgate East Underground. When
we pulled up in front of the building, I asked the driver to wait. "I'll only
be a second."

"The meter's running, mate."

I walked into the London Aid Society and was greeted by a red-haired
woman with big green eyes. "How can I help you?" she asked.

"I'd like to drop off a donation," I said.

"Oh, that's wonderful." She stood. "Let me get Mr. Briggs."

"No, no. I just want to drop it off. Can I leave it with you?"

She seemed confused at first, but then smiled. "Of course."

I gave her the envelope with my donation, then headed back outside. I
wanted to avoid Briggs. Like I said, I'm not good with goodbyes.

I climbed back into the taxi. "Next stop, Croydan Airport," I said.

The taxi pulled away from the curb and we were on our way.

A thought ran through my head. It was something Beckley had said
when I left, and I couldn't get it out of my mind. "It must feel good to be
going home," he had said. I nodded and agreed, but the truth was, I didn't

feel like I was going home. I had lived in the United States for the first twenty or so years of my life, and for most of that time, my father had made me feel unwelcome. As soon as I could, I got out.

Now that I was going back, I thought about my father. Would I see him when I got back to the States? I wasn't sure. I wondered what he had said in all those letters he sent. I never read any of the letters and I never set him a response, but he kept writing just the same.

I hadn't thought things through about where I was going to live or what I was going to do. All I knew was that I was going to the United States. I bought a ticket on a Pan Am flight to New York. I wasn't sure what came after that. Maybe I would stay in New York or maybe I would go back to Chicago. The only thing I knew for sure was that I'd eventually figure things out.

The only time I had felt at home in my entire life was when I was with Kimberly. All the years before and all the years after, I was lost, without a home. There was a part of me that wanted to mourn Kimberly forever, to never give her up. But I could not deny the fact that she was gone, and I was still here. Maybe what Mindy Parsons had said before our night together was right. Although I would remember and love Kimberly always, it was time to move on, to make a new life for myself. It wasn't disrespectful to Kimberly. It was necessary for me.

Section 4

United States
(1945-1948)

Chapter 60
(1946)

I heard someone call, and I shielded my eyes from the sun to see who it was. There was a guy across the street, and he was yelling at a woman, trying to get her attention. This was a common occurrence. Where London had been reserved, even genteel, despite the war and the damage done by German bombs, New York was boisterous and loud, something always happening.

I had rented an apartment in Greenwich Village, near a few jazz clubs that had popped up in recent years. I thought I might hook on at one of the clubs to play piano. Instead, I met a trumpeter named Ricky de Palma who had a band that traveled the east coast doing shows. They were looking for a piano player and I was looking for a job. A match made in heaven. Or so I hoped.

My apartment was small and not particularly nice. When I arrived in New York, I wasn't sure what the future held for me. Despite having Kimberly's money in the bank, I didn't want to spend too much on rent. I had a six-month lease on the apartment, which I thought would give me time to figure out whether or not I wanted to stay in New York.

While there, I took the opportunity to visit a doctor about my missing eye. The eye patch look had grown tired, and the doctor I saw fit me with a glass eye. When I looked in the mirror, I saw me, not the Piano Playing Pirate. It was a welcome change.

In Miami, we were doing the final show of the year when Ricky called us all together in his room. Ricky didn't have many meetings like this, so I was curious what might be on his mind.

"Nice room," Tommy Cole, our drummer whispered to me. He was talking about the fact that Ricky had a one-bedroom suite, while the rest of us doubled up in regular hotel rooms. Tommy was my roommate. "What do you think he wants with us?"

I don't know," I said. "Maybe he just wants to make sure we all know what time the bus is pulling out after our show tomorrow night."

Ricky stood in front of the room and quieted us down. His jet-black hair was slicked back, and he had a cocktail in his hand. From the sound of his voice, it wasn't his first of the day.

"I have an announcement to make," Ricky said. He took a sip of his drink and waited for everyone to stop talking. When we were quiet, he continued. "This will be our last show for a while. I think we all could use a break."

Several of the band members nodded their heads. We had been going hot and heavy for the past four months, and we could use a break. A few weeks off would help us all recharge our batteries. Christmas was just a couple weeks away, and it would be good to stay home until after the new year.

Charlie Demarco, our sax player, raised his hand as if he was a student in a classroom.

Ricky called on him. "Yeah, Charlie?"

"How long are we going to be home?" Charlie asked. "If I'm home too much, my old lady gets annoyed with me."

Charlie's comment brought a laugh.

Ricky looked uncomfortable. He took a big swig of his drink and waited for the laughter to die down.

"This is going to be a long break," he said. "We don't have any shows scheduled until the middle of April."

"What the hell?" somebody said.

"April?" Tommy said. "How are we supposed to make any money between now and April? I have bills to pay."

Several of the band members spoke at once, angry with Ricky for the long break. Ricky held up his hands to quiet us.

"I know. I know. It's a long break, "Ricky said. "But I think we could all use some time off. We'll plan rehearsals at the beginning of April and be back on the road a couple of weeks later."

"You don't pay us for time off or rehearsals, so we won't have a paycheck until late April," Tommy said. "How do you expect us to make ends meet until then?"

While the other bandmembers argued with Ricky, I stood and left the room. I wasn't in the mood for yelling and arguing. I understood why Tommy, Charlie, and the others were upset. Ricky didn't pay us much to begin with, but we counted on that money to pay our bills. Four months or more without pay wasn't an option for most of the guys.

My situation was a little different. I had some money in the bank, even if I didn't want to touch it, and I had been thinking about leaving New York anyway. My time with Ricky de Palma's band hadn't turned out to be what I had hoped, so I viewed our break as a chance to start over somewhere else. Where that would be, I didn't know.

I went to the hotel bar and ordered a beer. They didn't have Guinness, so I asked for a Pabst Blue Ribbon. It wasn't a bad beer, but it wasn't Guinness.

I had been thinking about going to Chicago to see my father. We hadn't spoken in more than twenty-five years. Maybe it was time to bury the hatchet. I still wasn't sure if it was a good idea or not, but I had been thinking about it.

A man slid onto the barstool next to me. "Are you Henry Ross?" he asked.

I didn't recognize the man, who was smartly dressed in a suit and tie. "I am," I said.

"I'm Paul Cantrill," he said. "I work for Louie Armstrong's management company."

I shook his hand. I knew all about Louie Armstrong, the trumpet player and bandleader. He had been part of King Oliver's Creole Jazz Band that played the first ever show at The Blue Note. He was a legend. "Nice to meet you," I said.

"I caught your show up in Fort Lauderdale," he said. "I enjoyed watching you play."

I thanked him for his comment. It was especially nice coming from someone who was involved with a jazz great like Louie Armstrong.

"I heard Ricky de Palma is shutting things down for a few months."

"Boy, bad news sure travels fast," I said.

Cantrill laughed. "I've actually known for a while. Ricky and his family are going to spend the winter in California. He called a few months ago to see if we knew about any rentals around L.A."

That explained Ricky taking a break. I should have known it had nothing to do with giving the band some much deserved time off.

"I want to run an idea by you," he said. "Louie is preparing to do a short tour in Cuba next month. It's been set up since last winter. But our piano player, Harley Grimes, can't make the trip. Since you're about to have a lot of time off, how would you like to sit in for the tour?"

Playing with Louie Armstrong, even if just for a short time, would be a real step up from playing with Ricky. There wasn't much to think about. "How many shows," I asked. I didn't want to seem overly anxious.

"We're going to start rehearsing right after Christmas. Then we have two warm up shows here in Florida the weekend after New Year's, then we go to Cuba for five shows. We'll be back home by the end of January."

I nodded my head and acted as if I was thinking. I already knew my answer.

"Of course, you'll be paid for rehearsals and all of the shows," he said.

"Sounds great," I said. "Count me in."

Chapter 61
(1947)

Playing with Louie Armstrong was everything I had hoped it would be. Louie was very kind to me, treating me like I was doing the band a huge favor to play with them. Of course, the opposite was true. I was grateful for the opportunity.

The tour of Cuba went too fast. I think we all enjoyed the experience, playing in front of crowds that knew and appreciated the music. The final show in Havana was a real barn burner. The energy was high, and we all seemed to recognize that the tour, although short, had been something very special.

After the show, I was approached by an older man with white hair and a beard. There was something familiar about him.

"Look at you," he said. "From jazz critic to jazz star."

I recognized that voice, but it took me a second to place it. "Ernest, how are you?" It was my old friend from Paris. In the years since I had last seen him, Ernest had aged significantly. He had also become one of the most popular writers in the world. I had read several of his books and had bragged to my former bandmates that I knew the famous writer, although I don't think any of them believed me.

"I'm as fine as frog hair." His voice was still deep and gruff. "Do you have plans tonight?"

"I was going to have a drink with some of my bandmates," I said. "We head back to the states tomorrow."

"I'm meeting some people over at El Floridita, just around the corner on Calle Obispo. Join us, will you?"

"Do you mind if I bring a few people with me?"

"The more the merrier," he said. "Don't be long. We have a lot of catching up to do."

Ernest rushed off and I gathered a few bandmates to join us at El Floridita. We walked to the bar through the sticky Havana night air.

Inside El Floridita, my bandmates went off in search of drinks and I went off in search of Ernest. He wasn't hard to find. I just had to follow the sound of the loudest voice in the bar. He was holding court at a table with four other men. I caught the end of the story he was telling. Something about chasing a German submarine. When he saw me, he said farewell to his tablemates and motioned for me to follow him. We went to the back of the bar where he spoke to a man sitting by himself at a small table. The man nodded agreeably with whatever Ernest was saying to him. When Ernest had finished talking, the man abandoned the table, and we sat down.

"I thought it would be easier to talk back here," he said.

Ernest had changed. He was as exuberant as ever, but he seemed sadder and less confident. I told him I had recently read For Whom the Bell Tolls and that I enjoyed it very much.

"Thank you, Henry. That means a lot coming from an old friend like you." A shadow seemed to cross his face and he exhaled deeply. "I'm not sure I have anything left to write," he said. "It feels like the well has run dry."

"That can't be true, Ernest. Maybe you just need a break." I wanted to sound supportive, but the truth was I had no idea what was going on with him.

"Maybe," he said. "Or maybe I need to go back to Key West. That's where my creative juices were really flowing."

One of the bartenders came to our table and asked "Mr. Hemingway" if he and his friend would like a drink. We each ordered beers, and the bartender went to fetch them for us.

We spent the next half hour talking about how much he loved Key West. He loved the bars, the fishing, the weather, and the lifestyle. He had friends there, and he said every time he visited, it felt like home. "I enjoy Cuba, but I miss Key West. If I hadn't divorced Pauline and married Martha, I would have never left."

I knew from reports I'd read in the newspaper that Ernest had married war journalist Martha Gellhorn. Their relationship had been big news.

"Is Martha here?" I glanced around the barroom.

Ernest shook his head and got a look on his face like he had tasted something sour. "No, she's in Algiers reporting on war profiters or some such nonsense." He took a gulp of his beer. "What about you, Henry? What have you been up to since we last spoke in Paris?"

I told him that I had married the woman he had met at The Ritz so long ago in Paris. The news excited him. He remembered her. I shared the story about Kimberly and Jimmy dying during the Blitz. It crossed my mind that it wasn't as painful as it once was to tell the story of their deaths more than four years later. I still missed them both desperately, but my time with them seemed like it had occurred in another lifetime to a different version of me.

"War is a bitch," he said.

Ernest seemed to want to say more, but we were interrupted by my bandmates. When they approached the table, Ernest's demeanor shifted. He became the gregarious bon vivant again. The guys from the band wanted to let me know they were heading back to the hotel, but Ernest talked them into having one more drink. He entertained them with story after story, about fishing for giant Marlin in the Gulf Stream off Cuba, being an ambulance driver in Italy during the first World War, and watching bullfights in Spain. Ernest was a different man when he had an audience. The doubts and regrets were gone, replaced by confidence and machismo. I had to admit I liked the private Ernest better.

We had an early flight back to Miami, so we finally said our goodbyes. Ernest and I shook hands, promising to stay in touch.

"If you get the chance, visit Key West," he said. "I think you'll like the lifestyle."

I told him I would. As we left El Floridita, I heard Ernest's voice again rise above the din.

Chapter 62
(1946)

My time in Cuba made me decide I did not want to spend the winter in New York. When we got back to the States, I gathered my things and got an apartment in Miami. I was going to have to find a new job anyway, and I thought I could do that just as easily in the warmth of Miami as in the bitter cold of New York.

Once I was moved into my Miami apartment, I made the decision to fly to Chicago to see my father. I had put it off long enough. I still had hard feelings toward the old man for exiling me, but after more than twenty-five years, I decided it was time to stop playing the victim. Time had passed and life marched on.

I had considered calling ahead but decided against it. I wanted us to do our talking face-to-face, not over the phone. I guess I wanted to surprise him; the prodigal son returning after a long exile in the wilderness.

I walked across the tarmac, the heat radiating from the asphalt. The move to Miami had been a good one, but now that winter had given way to spring, the temperature had become oppressive. I wasn't complaining, at least not yet, but I got a glimpse of what life in Miani was going to look like when summer arrived.

After landing in Chicago, I took a taxi to my hotel. It was getting late in the day, and I decided to get a good night's sleep before facing the old man. For dinner, I went to a place called Geno and Georgetti's. The taxi driver recommended it and said I should get the thick cut ribeye and a baked potato. I wasn't disappointed.

The next morning, I drove to my old neighborhood. The grand homes in the neighborhood somehow didn't seem so grand anymore. They were nice, but not as big and ornate as they were in my memory.

The taxi dropped me off in front of my old house. Like the houses around it, my father's home seemed smaller than I remembered. I had butterflies in my stomach. I knocked on the door and waited for my father or Margaret to answer.

When the door opened, a young woman—at least, younger than me—answered.

"Can I help you?" she asked.

I assumed she was my father's maid. "I'm here to see Joseph Ross. Is he in?"

The woman tilted her head and squinted her eyes. "Henry? Is that you?"

When she smiled, I recognized Sarah, my half-sister. The last time I saw her, she must have only been ten or twelve years old. "Yes, it's me."

Sarah put her hand up to her mouth and stared. "Oh my God. We didn't know if you were alive or dead."

"I'm alive." I stepped back, held my arms out to the side, and turned completely around, as if to prove my existence.

"I can see that." Sarah stared for a beat more, then seemed to come back to the moment. "Please, come in." She held the door open, and I entered my childhood home.

Sarah led me into my father's library, offered me a seat, and said she'd be right back. She quickly walked out of the room. I assumed she had gone to fetch my father.

I hadn't thought through what I wanted to say to him. In fact, there really was nothing I wanted to say. Whatever hurt he had caused me all those years earlier had faded. I'm not sure if I had forgiven him, but I wasn't interested in rehashing the past. What was done was done. He was now an old man, and it didn't make sense to reexamine his past behavior. Things had worked out okay for me. I no longer had the same hard feelings toward him.

Sarah returned to the room and took a seat opposite me in the other overstuffed chair. "I asked Lily to make some tea for us," she said. "I hope you like tea."

"I do," I said. "Who's Lily?"

"Oh, Lily is our housekeeper. She's been with us more than twenty years."

I nodded. A lot of time had passed since I'd last been in the house. It was only natural that a lot of things had happened to which I wasn't privy.

We sat quietly for a few moments before I broke the silence. "Is father here?" I asked.

Sarah sat on the edge of her chair and leaned forward. "No, Henry. I'm so sorry, but Father is…he's no longer alive."

I had assumed the old man was still living. I hadn't prepared myself for him being dead. "Oh, I didn't know," I said. "How long ago?"

"Three years," she said. "We tried to find you. His attorney hired a private investigator and they searched everywhere for you, but they came up empty."

"I was in England," I said.

"We had an address for you there. Father said he had written to you, but that you never answered his letters."

Before I could respond, Lily brought in the tea and poured us each a cup.

"Lily, I'd like you to meet Henry. Henry, this is Lily."

"It's nice to meet you, sir. I've heard a lot about you," Lily said.

"It's very nice to meet you, Lily." I didn't stand and I didn't offer to shake her hand. That was common, even expected. Yet, I silently cursed myself for my poor behavior.

Lily was rotund and had dark, brown skin. Seeing her reminded me of Sally. She also reminded me of my friend Eugene. I hadn't heard anything about him in more than two decades. I didn't even know if he had survived the war.

Sarah thanked Lily, and the housekeeper left the room. I added a splash of milk and a sugar cube to my tea and gently stirred it.

"It's been a very long time, Henry. Maybe you should tell me what has happened to you since we last saw you."

I shared the highlights of what had happened to me during the past thirty or so years. Sarah listened politely while she drank her tea. When I finished, I took a sip of my tea and realized it had gone cold. I put my cup on the table.

"You've lived quite a life. I'm so sorry about Kimberly and Jimmy," she said. "Let me tell you what has happened here." Sarah set her cup on the table and seemed to be preparing herself to recount the past few decades.

"Father died at his office in 1943 from a heart attack. Roger was working with him at the office and found him."

I nodded. "How is Roger?"

"Roger is doing well. He's married and has four children. He still works at father's office. He's a partner now. He's on a business trip in New York at the moment."

It probably wasn't fair, but it sounded to me like Roger was doing the job I would have been doing if things had turned out differently. Of course, would I have been happy doing that job? Probably not. Maybe things worked out for the best.

"How is your mother?" I asked.

"She has good days and bad days," Sarah said. "After my husband died…" she paused a moment when she saw the look of confusion on my face.

"My husband, Tim, died during the war. He was killed on D-Day."

"I'm sorry, Sarah. I guess the war took something from both of us."

Sarah nodded and looked down at her hands, which were in her lap. "I guess so." She took a moment, then continued. "When Tim died, the kids and I—I have two kids—we moved in with Mom. We've been here ever since. A few years ago, Mom started forgetting things. It was little things at first, but now, there are days she doesn't know who I am. The doctors recommended putting her in a nursing home, but I can't do that to her. We can take care of her here."

It had been good seeing Sarah, but I barely knew her, and I suddenly felt like I was intruding on a home and family where I didn't belong. My only connection to this family was my father. And with him gone, that connection was broken.

I thanked Sarah for the tea and told her it had been good catching up, but that I needed to run.

Sarah seemed to understand. She was probably as uncomfortable as I was.

"Before you go, I have something for you." She crossed the room to my father's desk and pulled a business card out of the top drawer. "This is the law firm that Father was using when he died. They're the ones that were looking for you. Father left something for each of us when he died, including you. You should call them."

I wasn't sure what to say. Perhaps I was in shock. First, I found out that my father had died three years earlier, and then I learned there had been something—I wasn't sure what—waiting for me. "Right. I'll give them a call."

I offered Sarah my hand, but she ignored it and hugged me. "It was good seeing you, Henry. I'm glad you're okay."

I hugged her awkwardly, then left the home that held so many unhappy memories for me.

Chapter 63
(1946)

The attorney's name was Andrew Marsden. He was tall and thin, with a head full of gray hair and a sharp beak-like nose. He reminded me of an eagle. Despite his rather fierce appearance, he was soft spoken and friendly.

Marsden was surprised to see me. He said they had been looking for me for two years after my father's death. When they couldn't find me, they finally gave up.

"I knew your father for many years, and we had several conversations about you," he said. "Your father could be a complicated man. He was a genius at business, but wasn't very good at the normal, everyday things, like raising a son. He told me that after your mother died, he didn't know what to do with you. He wanted to be a good father, but his grief over losing your mom and brother was so great he couldn't seem to get past it. When he met and married Margaret, he felt like he finally had a chance to move on with his life."

"Except for me," I said.

Marsden smiled. "Except for you. You were not only a reminder of his old life—the life he had lost—but he saw you as a personification of his grief. With you around, he didn't feel he could get past the grieving and move on with his life."

I nodded. In a strange way, I understood what my father was going through. I had a horrible time getting over my grief with Kimberly. Everything reminded me of her, and when it did, the grief came roaring back. I still struggled with it. I understood how my father grieved every time I reminded him of what had happened to my mother and Philip.

"The thing is, shipping you off to college and away from home turned his feelings of grief into feelings of guilt. He felt guilty for having sent you away, and he carried that guilt around with him until the day he died."

I didn't know what to say. The old man had done the best job he could with the cards he'd been dealt. I could see now that he didn't blame me for the deaths of my mother and brother. I was just a reminder of their deaths and the grief he felt over losing them.

I was beginning to see my entire childhood in a different light, and the change made me uncomfortable. I had misunderstood my father and how he felt about me for years. Seeing it in a new light made me want to cry. And the urge to cry made me want to leave.

I stood up and thanked Marsden for his time.

"Wait a minute," he said. "I have some paperwork for you to sign. We've been waiting years to get this done."

I sat down. Marsden pushed a button on his phone and asked the person on the other end to bring in the Joseph Ross file.

When the file was delivered, Marsden took several pages of documents out of the file and arranged them into three stacks on the desk. He pointed to where I had to sign, and when I was done, he said, "Congratulations, Henry. You're significantly wealthier now than you were when you walked in here."

I had signed where I was told to sign, but I had no idea what the signatures were all about. "I am? What the hell did I just sign?"

"Your father left you sixty thousand dollars in 1943, and it's been in the bank earning interest ever since. That's what the papers said that you signed."

I was stunned. I thought of all the things I could do with that money. I had been looking for a change, and the money made that change possible. For whatever reason, I got an image of Ernest in my mind, and I remembered what he had said about Key West. Maybe I could find change there.

Chapter 64
(1948)

The boat rocked back and forth in the gentle breeze. I cast my line out toward a small cove that looked like it might hold a fish or two. I twitched the line as I reeled it in, hoping to attract the attention of a big fish.

The early morning Florida sun shone down on me and my little boat. It was going to be another hot one today, but the morning air was comfortable, if not cool.

Ernest had been right. There was something magical about the Florida Keys. They were a world unto themselves. But rather than settle in his beloved Key West, I opted to live on Cudjoe Key, far enough away from Key West to avoid the crowds and higher house prices, but close enough to enjoy all Ernest's old home had to offer.

I felt a tick on the line and waited patiently for the fish to decide if he was going to eat my bait or not. There was another tick, then another. I leaned forward toward the fish, then pulled back hard. The hook set.

The fish took off toward the mangroves, but I kept pressure on the line; enough to control the fish but not enough to break it off. The fish fought for several minutes, but I made headway, reeling it ever closer to the boat. About ten feet from the boat, the fish jumped, and I saw it was a snook.

It made another run when it got close to the boat, but it was tiring. I reeled it in and reached down to grab the fish by the lower lip. I pulled it into the boat and marveled at the silver sleekness of it. I took the hook out of its mouth and placed it back in the water. Snook, cooked properly, can be delicious. But I already had a freezer full. No need to keep this one.

The fish was lethargic, exhausted from his fight and its time in the boat. I moved it back and forth in the water, running water through its gills, reviving it. It took a moment, but the fish regained its energy and swam away from the boat, slowly at first, then it quickly darted away.

I leaned against the seat back and turned my face to the sun. My skin had tanned nicely in the time I had lived on Cudjoe Key. It was hard not to be tan down here, but I wasn't complaining. Life was good.

I started the boat's motor and headed back to land. A twist of the throttle on the outboard engine and the bow rose up, cutting a "V" through the flat, shallow water. As I skimmed across Florida Bay between Cudjoe and Summerland Keys, the early morning haze receded, allowing the sun to fully break through. I sighed and counted myself lucky to be in this peaceful place, away from the death and destruction that had invaded my life in London.

At home, I tied the boat to the dock and grabbed my fishing poles and tackle box. The grass between the dock and the house was dewy, dampening my salt-covered huaraches. Inside the screened-in porch, I stored the fishing rods and tackle box in the corner, removed my wet sandals, and went inside.

"Welcome home," Teresa said.

I smiled and crossed the kitchen to kiss her. "Good morning."

I met Teresa one night at Mallory's. I was playing piano, something I still did on occasion, and she was with a group of friends. We hit it off. She had a cottage in Key West, but often woke up at my place.

"Want some breakfast?" she asked.

"You're reading my mind," I said.

"If I can do that, you'd better watch what you think." She slapped me on the butt.

I kissed her again. "I'm going to take a quick shower."

In the bathroom, the hot water ran over my head and cascaded down my body. I turned my back to the showerhead and wiped my face. It had been years since I had felt so content. I stood in the warm spray and felt cocooned away, safe from the heartbreak and tragedy I'd experienced in another place, another life.

"Breakfast is ready," Teresa called.

I didn't know what the future might hold, but at least for now, this was home. However long it might last—a week, a year, ten years—I was determined to enjoy it.

Acknowledgements

I am fortunate to have many people helping me during the writing process and I'd like to thank them all. I truly appreciate their support, comments, suggestions, and patience.

In particular, as always, I'd like to thank my kids, Shelby and Louis. Their love empowers me and I am extremely proud of them both.

I'd also like to thank my editor, Sean Ironman. His work made this book infinitely better once he got his hands on it. I am thankful for his friendship and his willing counsel.

Amy Zizich Beyer, the world's greatest proofreader, found all of my mistakes, even after I was convinced there were no more to find. Thank you, Amy!

I was fortunate to have Jessica Barrett and Clay Snellgrove read over my manuscript before it saw the light of day. Their thoughts and suggestions were incredibly helpful. Thank you both.

About the Author

Lou Mindar is the author of *The Ones That Got Away*, *Driven: A Novel* and the novella collection, *Road Stories*. He is a graduate of Western Illinois University and received his MFA in creative writing from the University of Central Florida. He lives in Wisconsin and Florida.

For updates about new releases, as well as exclusive promotions, visit the author's website at www.LouMindar.com.